ODETTE

ODETTE

ALEXEY WILLIAMS

Your worst sin is that you have destroyed and betrayed yourself for nothing.

Fyodor Dostoevsky

1

The men drove the horses onto the freight car, and the freight car swallowed them. Behind them, the pumpjacks and grain elevators. The horse dealer had given himself ample time to drive the horses onto the freight, but things never seemed to go as planned. I helped the men, though the horse dealer hadn't asked me. I was coming back from bronc riding, and I had the time. The main issue was that the freight car wasn't attached properly to the rest of the train. The horses didn't seem to mind. They were working horses. Only when the car finally hitched with a clang did they whinny. They were still whinnying when I climbed the car and approached the bars to get a better look at them. They had sleek bodies. One of them, a mare, approached my open hand. "That one's called Dancing Lady," the horse dealer said. "She got her coloring from her dam."

After the train stopped, Jean got out and walked into the parking lot. Her body was correct in her frilly dress. It was a green dress that had the image of horses galloping across a field. Jean was looking away when I approached her in the parking lot. She was looking at the pumpjacks. I raised my hat and smoothed my hair with a hand. I asked her if she needed any help. I told her I managed the main ranch outside town. She knew where that was. I mentioned that she'd probably forgotten me.

"I haven't forgotten you," she said.

We walked together. The road was seldom paved, though it had been when we started. We saw the silos on the abandoned farms and the roads that led from one abandoned farm to another. At times we heard the clop of horse hooves on the ground. These were feral horses. Jean drew nearer to me as she walked along, and I knew she would be perfect for what Miss Bouverie wanted her for. Jean told me about her hemophilia. I wouldn't have known if she hadn't told me. We passed a woman sitting unhappily on a porch with her children. They were all sweating in the heat of early summer.

When we reached Jean's sister's place, I told Jean that they were hiring on the ranch I managed. I managed one permanent hand and whatever seasonal workers the owner hired. She'd be a maid in the owner's house if she wanted. It'd be easy work. Jean maneuvered her auburn hair to one side of her neck with her hand as girls do. Then we heard the clamor of cattle being driven into town.

When I reached the house, I saw the cattle doctors examining two steers on the grass. A steer is a castrated male bull. Huntley and I had been separating the steer pairs the day before, and we had taken out these two for doctoring. We couldn't properly doctor them ourselves. I walked into the house and soon reached the second floor. From a window in the hall, I could see into Miss Bouverie's house, which was immediately adjacent to ours. Two lone houses sitting far back on the ranch. I passed Huntley's room. There was a men's magazine lying atop his bed. In it was a story about a bronc rider named Jesse. Jesse wasn't his real name. Jesse understood the life of roping and castrating because he'd lived it. I knew Jesse's story because I'd read the magazine. There were a man's heavy boots peeking out from under the bed. Huntley had trained as a farrier, and there were horseshoeing instruments on the dresser. I heard Huntley's boots thud up the stairs. He butted roughly into me, resting one of his hands briefly on my hip when he reached me. He asked me what I was looking in his room for. "Goddamn you," he said. He charged inside the bedroom and slammed the door.

It was silent in Miss Bouverie's house when I entered, and the lady herself was sitting up in bed when I reached her bedroom. "There you are," she said. Her Colt Python clanked on a bedside table. The eight-inch Colt Python has a long neck like a swan.

Miss Bouverie managed to sit up completely only after I'd helped her. She had no use of her legs and was frail everywhere. When she was sat up, she smoothed the sides of her pinned-up hair. She told me she needed me to go into town tomorrow to see about selling thirty head of cattle. Fifteen pair. She said she could get Hunt to go if I didn't want to.

"I found someone," I told Miss Bouverie. "A young woman."

"Then bring her to the ranch so I can see her. She can stay in the house with me. What did you say her name was?"

"Her name's Jean," I told her.

Miss Bouverie glanced out the window as if recollecting what the pumpjacks were for.

"Are we gonna hurt her?" I asked.

"Yes," said Miss Bouverie.

I left Miss Bouverie's room after that. The next day I went to town on that business about the cattle. I'd decided to meet Kirk. He was sitting in Vita's, and I told him he needed to come to the ranch to talk business with the owner. I said: "I need you to buy thirty head of cattle. The owner wants to sell." Kirk told me she only had 180 head on the whole ranch, which I knew. If anyone ought to know how many cattle there were, it would be the man who managed the ranch. Kirk told me I had a hitch in my get-along as he'd just bought cattle off a ranch that had shut down and he was short on cash. But I told Kirk he could promise to pay now but pay later like how they used to do back in the day. He only had to sign something. Kirk agreed to buy the thirty head and then stop at the ranch to complete the sale. I called the ranch phone, but no one answered. I'd left Huntley to tend the cattle with another man. A seasonal worker. It wasn't hard work as the land was all fenced in. Roping, branding, castrating. Kirk grinned at me as I returned to the bar from the payphone, pushing his cowboy hat further down on his head. He didn't fancy wearing cowboy hats, but he wore them when dealing with the cattlemen. He knew the cattlemen preferred dealing with one of their own. Or at least someone they thought of as one of their own. We talked for a time. We talked about nothing as men do. Then I called Jean at her sister's. She answered the phone right away and the softness in her voice was like being someplace where there were only horses. She'd promised to cook supper but said we could meet afterward if I was still in town. But we didn't meet that day.

We met after Kirk suggested I invite Jean to the ranch. We'd all three drive to a creek that sat far back in the woods and have a roast. A man had taught Kirk how to roast meat on skewers over an open fire. You just staked a skewer through a large cut of meat and leaned it over the flame. After we reached the property and set everything up, Kirk and I sat on the bare ground, but Jean sat on a saddle blanket that I'd brought with us. When she'd seen me take it out of the pickup and sling it over my shoulder, she'd asked me what it was for. I told her it was just for sitting on. Her smooth legs were pretty against the red-gold of the saddle blanket. She cradled a bottle of mercurochrome in her hands. She watched as Kirk and I tested the skewered meat: cutting pieces off with a knife to see if the meat was done. It wasn't long before Kirk told us it was. He sliced some pieces from the shank and handed them to me. I made sure the meat wasn't too hot before I handed the pieces to Jean. I didn't know if burning her fingers could cause a problem with her hemophilia. When we were done, we returned to the pickup where we saw the lights of another truck driving towards us. I'd left the steroids in the back of the pickup. Stopping his truck, the driver got out and ran towards us. He mistook me for someone else and shouted at me. "Troy!" he shouted. "Troy!" I drew my Colt and took aim. The man stopped dead in his tracks. I raised the .45 into the air and fired. Bang. Jean ran to me. She wrapped an arm around my waist as the man slunk back to his truck. That's when I knew I had her. She was attired differently today. She had been pretty before, but now she seemed to belong to the landscape: the roads that led nowhere and would always do so.

2

We noticed a bruise on Jean's calf when we dropped her off at her sister's. Jean said she was fine, but I was worried about her hemophilia, so I swept her up and carried her into her sister's place. Jean was laughing and grinning. After I set her down, I got on my knees and kissed her bruise. She said she didn't know anything about me, so I showed her a Polaroid of Wrexham Jones, my grandfather. He was huddled together with some other men at the end of the Korean War.

3

Hannah lived on the land she'd inherited from her grandfather who had fought in the Korean War. The land here was wooded and grim, but when I saw Hannah running towards me happily it seemed different. The grass was so high it came up almost to her knees. On the back of Hannah's lot was the old Dodge that couldn't be driven anymore and in front of that was the house. The horses meandered on the lawn that surrounded the house. These were the two horses that Hannah had wanted me to see. I told her it wouldn't do any good. These horses hadn't been tamed properly when they were colts, and they didn't like to be ridden. Hannah stopped running suddenly when she reached me. She reached her hands out to me. I took them and I looked into her dark brown eyes. She asked me if I remembered when she had built the house. I had been working at the textile mill then, and after that I worked for the newspaper. The textile mill wasn't far away from where Hannah lived. We both searched for it with our gaze in the light of the morning.

Max, a neighbor of Hannah's, waved at us as we got into the pickup. He was a giant with humongous hands. I told Hannah that she should tie the horses up, but she said they'd be all right. Max would watch them. And if they got away, he would bring them home. As we drove off, one of the horses lowered its head and chewed on the grass. Hannah smoothed a crinkle in her dress. Then she turned to look out the pickup's passenger-side window.

"She'll be angry you're gone," Hannah said.

"Who do you mean?"

"Miss Bouverie. Isn't that her name?"

"Is that who you're looking for out the window?"

"No."

"I didn't realize you knew her," I said.

"I don't," Hannah said. "It's a small place, Kip. Even if I'm not exactly in the same town."

When the pickup rolled over an unexpected bump in the road, Hannah jumped in her seat. She laughed in the carefree way that was hers alone. "Who is she?" she asked. I shook my head as I didn't know who she meant. We passed the small Catholic church where Hannah and I had attended mass once a month, even though I wasn't a Catholic. The priest there ministered to the migrant workers.

When we reached the small village Hannah called a town, she hopped smiling out of the pickup. She was happier than she'd been when we lived together. She told me she was sorry. "Sorry for what?" I asked her. But she couldn't say. I went with her into the notary's office where a portly woman notarized the documents that I'd signed. Although we were separated, we were technically still married. And as Hannah had recently inherited some property from a brother, she needed me to sign certain things. I often saw her looking out of the window of the pickup at the blank landscape. She understood that no matter how far a horse ran it never got anywhere.

Hannah had brought a leather case to put her notarized documents into. She said she wanted to stop at the bank and then we could drive back home. We'd lived in that house for most of the time we were married. Hannah had it built with my wages from the mill, and when it was finished we lived there. Then I worked at the paper. The Spaulding County Press Herald. Hannah produced a pack of cigarettes as she walked out of the bank building. I saw the workers in the bank watching us as we drove off. "Light one for me, would you?" Hannah said. "I told you I quit, but it wasn't true. I did try." She offered me a cigarette, but I didn't take one as I didn't smoke anymore. She was still puffing out smoke when the pickup ground to a stop at the only stoplight in town.

"You planning on telling me who she is?" Hannah asked as the pickup neared the woods behind her house.

The wooded part of her neighborhood was the only part of the land that wasn't flat. The tops of the evergreens pierced the sky and unleveled the landscape.

"Who is she? What's her name?"

"You're asking me what Miss Bouverie's first name is?"

"No, I'm asking you the name of the woman you're sleeping with," and Hannah turned to face me at last. "You seem to be suggesting it's Miss Bouverie."

I told Hannah that Miss Bouverie could hardly be sleeping with anyone as she was a known invalid. When we reached Hannah's house, I jabbed hard on the brake to avoid hitting a horse. One of those goddamned horses that Hannah hadn't wanted to tie up. Hannah and I got out of the pickup and walked towards the house. When we reached the door, I told Hannah that I ought to put the horses in the stable shed behind the house. It gave me a chance to get a better look at them. And I didn't like the thought that they might run off and never be seen or heard of again. Back in the house, in the living room, we heard the horses neighing in the stable shed. We heard the sound of Hannah's tenant, Martha, who lived upstairs. Hannah told me that this girl was in a fight with her boyfriend on the telephone. Martha was always in a fight with her boyfriend on the telephone. I told Hannah that I had to go wash my hands.

When I returned, Hannah told me that I was looking better. She thought I was looking better through my clothes. She thought I looked strong. "Are you taking stuff again?" she asked. I told her I was back on equipoise and winstrol, and she said that she could tell. Hannah walked to the mirror. It was just a high mirror that hung in a corner of the living room. She pulled her dark hair away from her long neck and admired herself. She was too slim, but she was still pretty. And it didn't matter what I thought. I stood beside Hannah in front of the mirror. She guided my hand to a place on her thin slip of a waist. She placed a hand atop my shoulder, and we danced like that for a minute. As we danced, I glanced into the mirror. At first, it was Hannah that I saw dancing with me in the mirror's reflection, but after a while her face and shape changed into that of Miss Bouverie. She had taken down her pinned-up hair. Miss Bouverie looked well and back to her former self. She broke free from our dancing embrace in the mirror. Turning to face Hannah, she reached both hands out of the mirror and brought them to Hannah's neck. She tightened her hands, strangling Hannah.

4

As Jean was settling into her room, I went to the lawn to work on Huntley's pickup. I'd heard a series of clicks when I was driving it earlier. I worked on the vehicle bare-chested, bending over and getting dried oil all over me. I had the hood up. I had it up on those narrow poles like you do. It's always strange that they don't give. I knew Jean was watching me from the window. At one point, Jean walked away from the window and made for the door to her room. Someone must have knocked. I heard a pair of voices through the windowpanes. But Jean came back to the window after the person left. She came to watch me working on the car shirtless, and I pretended not to notice.

Outside, the cattle doctors examined two steers. They'd come back, and these were a different pair of steers than those they had seen before. The steers were so thin you could see their ribs through their heavy coats. One of the doctors used a metal instrument to open the mouth of one of the steers. "The gums are purple," he said, turning to look at the other doctor. I was near enough to where they were that I could turn to glance at them occasionally even though I was working on Huntley's truck. The steers were sick and seemed to take no notice of the two men. As a boy, I had been told that a cow's vision is two to three times better than that of a man.

About three days after Jean was brought on, I was walking past Miss Bouverie's room when I heard the lady laugh. She and Jean were laughing together like two girls sitting in the back of church. But Miss Bouverie's laugh was different from Jean's. Miss Bouverie's laugh was like that of the oilman who knew that there'd never be a time when oil wasn't needed. There would never be a place. As they chatted and laughed together, I noted the contents of the room. There were the new flowers laid flat on the table by the door. There was the Colt sitting atop the bedside table. There was the Colt's leather holster. The legs of a toy horse could be seen from beneath the bed. The toy horse was lying on its side. I heard the wind lashing against the window.

I heard the wind lashing loudly the night the rain returned. It had rained hard. But it had been a good day. Babette, the cook, had told me that Miss Bouverie was pleased with Jean. Miss Bouverie was feeling worse, and Jean always attended her in her bedroom. Babette brought her meals there, and Miss Bouverie and Jean would eat together. Late that night, I heard the patter of footsteps on the hall. I heard when the door into my room creaked open. The wood planks of the floor were wide and warped. They creaked like donkeys braying. Sometimes when the steers were sick, they made a noise like donkeys braying. The footsteps neared my bed, and then I felt when the sheet was pulled up and the woman, whoever she was, got into bed with me. The mattress hardly moved since someone small-framed had gotten into it. I was dressed only in my underwear. I felt the woman's hand on my shoulder. I felt it on my leg. Her grip was tight, and it felt like I belonged to her.

Later I learned from Miss Bouverie that she needed me to drive to Thibault County to pick up a mare that she'd bought. As she said this, she sat up higher in the bed as if saying something important. Jean was in the room with us. Miss Bouverie had decided to get into horse rearing, like her daddy had done. She'd take this mare she'd bought and breed it with others. She said she'd get all new horses to breed. She told me that I'd need someone to go along with me, since they'd have to drive the truck back to the ranch as I'd be driving the horse transport. I thought she'd say Huntley, but she told me he was needed about the place. Someone had to tend to the cattle. She decided that Jean should go.

"You do now how to drive, don't you?" she asked Jean.

When we walked into the diner, we saw the sky coming through in the easy colors of the late afternoon. The men in the pickup that had followed us for the better part of ten miles didn't come inside with us. They got out of their truck, walked to the door, and then walked right back to the pickup. Jean hadn't noticed them. She wanted a booth near the kitchen, far from the windows. I said that this was the worst place to sit in the diner as you always had waitresses coming past you with another person's food. Jean didn't mind. The waitresses were all young. Their shapely legs were visible through their sheer stockings. They wore white tennis shoes and had small red bows in their hair. Jean didn't say that she was happy to be away from Miss Bouverie. She was too polite to, but I could tell all the same. We were both hunched over our menus when the waitress came back to take our orders.

"We should have spoken about where we'd stay tonight," I said as the waitress searched her pockets for a pencil.

"Shh. She's ready," said Jean. "It'll be fine."

"I'm ready," said the waitress.

She was a young girl twirling her curly blond hair with a finger. She took our orders. Two steak burgers with fries on the side. "No fries," Jean said as the waitress walked away. She'd changed her mind. Then a bell chimed when a couple walked into the diner. A high-school-aged girl in a pleated skirt came in with her boyfriend. The boy was burly and bouncing off the walls as if powered by Rayovac batteries. He put an arm around the girl's waist.

"You think she's pretty?" Jean asked softly.

"Yeah, but not as pretty as you," I said.

The waitress returned with our drinks. Mine was a root beer in a Mason jar. They served all their drinks in Mason jars. Jean's was a water. The sky was dark when we left the diner. The two men that had trailed us still sat in the parking lot in their vehicle. When I revved the engine to Hunt's pickup, I heard the driver of their pickup power his engine too. "Do you know them?" I asked Jean. She shook her head but didn't say anything. It was dark, but we still made out the declining, gray-blue sky of West Texas. A sky that doesn't know whether it wants to be in the USA or Mexico. "People are the same every-where," my grandfather used to say. There must be people like Miss Bouverie even in Mexico.

I found a motel two exits away from the diner. The men in the pickup made the same turn off that we did. Same old story. Local roughnecks with nothing to do. I told Jean they'd go away when they got bored or someone more interesting came into town. We saw the manager of the motel appear from a back room when we walked into the motel office. He was separated from us by bulletproof glass. Jean had brought her suitcase, even though we weren't going to be gone but two days. She set it down on the laminate floor as the manager nodded for me to approach. Just then, the men from the pickup came in behind us, but I knew they weren't renting a room. Jean drew closer to me. It was like instinct. She raised my arm up and dropped it over her shoulder.

"Two rooms, please," I told the man.

"No, one room with two beds," said Jean.

"A room with double beds?" the man asked.

"Yes, sir," said Jean.

The motel rooms all opened off a long colonnade outside. A staircase near the motel office led up to the third floor, where Jean and I would be. The men that had followed us disappeared back into their pickup and the motel manager vanished into his back room. Far behind the bulletproof glass. The first thing you saw when you came into the motel room was a mirror. I saw there the shape of my muscular form and Jean's slender one. The two beds were low and close together. The room didn't have the persistent cattle smell of the ranch. Jean plopped her suitcase on one of the beds and immediately began removing her things. I was facing away from her, look-ing for the television remote, but when I turned around, she smiled at me. She was just then taking a white dress out of the suitcase.

"I thought I'd wear this," she said. "This was the dress I was wearing before, when I went with you and Kirk to the ranch. Do you remember?"

"I do," I answered.

I found the remote but dropped it when I heard the sound of a car horn honking outside in the lot. I parted the blinds with two fingers. I saw a blue car with its lights on, but I didn't recognize it. I couldn't see the driver. I opened the door to go out, but Jean said: "No, don't. Who are they?" I told her it wasn't the men from before. It was someone else. "Did you bring your gun?" she asked. I told her I had, but it wasn't noth-ing to worry about. I could feel the heft of the gun holster against my upper thigh. The ends of my flannel shirt hid the holster from view.

I walked the stairs down to the parking lot. Rob was getting out of his car as I neared. "I didn't see you," I told him. I walked past Rob and his Ford to Huntley's pickup, where the product was. I got the veterinary steroids out of the truck and returned to Rob. I had bovine growth hormone and equipoise, which is a horse steroid. Human males took equipoise too, which gave them a lean, veiny look without retaining too much water. Winstrol could make you hold water. I handed the boxes to Rob. He didn't check the boxes to make sure the vials were all in there. He shoved the boxes into a bag he carried. Then he pushed a stack of bills in my hands. He returned to the car and backed his car out of the lot without a word. The bills were new and they had that new bill scent.

I returned to the truck for another box of horse steroids, and I took that up to the room along with a box of syringes. I realized that the men that'd been following us had gone when I reached the stairs. They must have gotten scared when they saw me talking to Rob. Rob was a big, ominous-looking person. I'd ridden broncs on the circuit with Rob years ago. Jean opened the door as I neared the room. She must have heard the tap of my shoes on the concrete walkway. The walkway was bowed as it if had been resurfaced many times. Jean looked like she had something to say, but she didn't say anything. I nodded at her as if I understood. She returned to her bed. She'd chosen the double bed furthest from the door. She picked up the remote but didn't change the channel. She laughed at the silly show on TV. I walked over to the mirror, which hung in a nook near the bathroom door. It was an old mirror with black marks where the surface was scratched away, but I could still see myself. I unbuttoned my flannel shirt and hung it on a rung tacked to the wall. I looked myself over and then I opened the box of equipoise. I called Jean over. As I drew the steroid into a syringe, I explained to her how to inject it and where to. The shoulder was a good spot, but since Jean hadn't done it before I decided on the buttock. The right buttock. I removed my holster and gun and then I unbuttoned my belt. I pulled down the waist of my jeans and the elastic of my underwear, and I bent forward a bit so Jean could have good access to the injection site. I laughed, but Jean only smiled.

When I woke up later, I found that Jean had gotten into bed with me. The bed wasn't large enough for two people, but Jean was so slender. She nestled in the space between my arm and my torso, and she said: "You're like a fast, sleek animal. Really, really fast." I told her that was a silly thing to say. She readjusted herself in bed and her hair fell over my arm. I asked her why she wanted a room with double beds if she planned to get in bed with me, and she said she didn't know. The TV prattled on. The host of the nighttime talk show laughed in a fake way, and it was like roasting in the ninth circle of hell. Just really grating. Jean still wore the virginal dress she had put on before. Her Mary Jane shoes rest underneath the bed. She glanced at me once, and then she looked away. She said: "I can't have children." She didn't tell me how she knew; she only told me that she couldn't. I pulled her closer to me and she cried. I felt her tears against the long, muscular crease in my chest.

Noreen was waiting for us on the steps up to her large house. She was the woman that owned the mare we'd come to get. I hadn't met her before, but I'd heard her mentioned many times. She was a tall woman with dark brown hair. Her hair was cut to a point somewhat below her ears. She looked like a TV actress. When I brought the truck to a stop, she walked the last couple of steps down from her house to the dry grass. She did this politely and in greeting, as someone very old-fashioned would do. Jean and I stepped out of the pickup, but Jean didn't approach the lady immediately. She waited for me to begin to walk and then she followed. The woman reached a hand out to me when I reached her. After we shook hands, she said: "Oh, that's a strong, manly shake." She smiled at me in what I thought was a natural way. She nodded at Jean. Then she turned and began walking back to the house.

"I'm so glad that you could come today," she said. "I know that you came for the mare, but I thought you could sit for a while and talk with me. I'm alone here. I'm basically alone."

The woman led us past the dusty portraits on the wall. We were in the house now. The floor didn't have a rug, and the woman's shoes tapped loudly as she led us to the kitchen.

"We'll sit in here," she said. "I hope you don't mind." I pulled out a chair for Jean, then my own, and we both sat across from the woman. The latter wore a thin dress that suited the humid weather. Her areolas were visible through the thin fabric of the dress. She generally smiled at us when she spoke. Outside, we could see the horses grazing on a field that sloped down to the house.

"The mare is in the stable," she said. "She isn't one of the horses grazing there."

"You have nice horses, Ma'am," I remarked. "I imagine you have many."

"I did once," the lady said. "Not anymore. I've been selling some. And I have a horse I need to put down. You might be able to help me with that. Do you have a gun?"

I told the lady that I did. Shortly afterward, a maid appeared. She looked surprised to see us. "It's okay, Gladys. Just put the coffeemaker on. We'll have some coffee."

Gladys busied herself in a corner of the kitchen until we completely forgot about her. Noreen had this way of looking at you. She looked frequently at me as she spoke, but rarely at Jean. When she did look at Jean, there was something fierce in her eyes like she wanted to tear the skin off of Jean's face with her fingers. The pretty, translucent skin of Jean's face. When the coffee was done, Noreen told Jean and me to follow her out back where she had lawn furniture for times like these. It was the expensive sort of lawn furniture that's made of iron and painted white. Noreen's dress was white like Jean's. Noreen sipped her coffee through a straw. She didn't have any sugar with it, but a lot of cream. She said she got the cream from a man that lived down the road. Down the road for her was thirty miles.

The men that worked about the place emerged from the stable. There was a younger man with a sharp, hungry look and an older man whose face was obscured by a wide-brimmed, patchwork hat. They didn't seem to have much to do just then. They meandered over to a gelding, spoke for a while, and then walked a different way. Noreen said that the horse she had sold to Miss Bouverie was the perfect breeding mare. She wasn't the horse that she was having troubles with. It didn't seem that Noreen understood what it meant to have troubles. She told us that there used to be many purebred horse breeders in Thibault County, but not anymore. She said that we would stay the night, and tomorrow she would take us to see the horseracing venue for two-year geldings that she had built. I told her we couldn't stay, as we were expected back at the Bouverie place that very night. She wouldn't hear it. She swatted me away like a fly that settles on your shoulder.

She told us that we would stay in guest bedrooms, which were off a hall in the back of the house on the second floor. She said that we had some time before supper. We could wander about the farm, and one of the men would fetch us when supper was served. She had her supper early. She told us later that it was the only meal she ate.

As the time for supper neared, I took off my shirt to change into the one that I had washed by hand in the bathroom. But the shirt hadn't dried yet so I didn't have a shirt to put on. I walked shirtless into Jean's room, which was separated from mine by an inner door. Jean was sitting in front of a vanity mirror applying her makeup. She had a way of putting on makeup that made it look like she wasn't wearing any at all. A brush swept the surface of Jean's face. I turned to walk back to my room when Jean was done. She followed me. She looped her arm into mine. She said: "It's strange that there are these things called steroids that can make you look like Superman." I laughed and told her it wasn't true. It's just she wasn't used to being around people that looked like me. When she spent more time around me, it wouldn't be so surprising to her.

I put my shirt on, though it still wasn't dry. I went down with Jean to the first floor where supper would be served. We met Logan, the younger of the stable hands, at the foot of the stairs. He told us that supper wouldn't be ready for another hour as it was only four o'clock. Logan was handsome, and as soon as I realized how handsome he was I wanted to take Jean away from there. He could ruin Miss Bouverie's plans. But Jean hardly seemed to notice. Logan directed us to the stables, and we found the other horses there. There was the mare that Miss Bouverie had bought. It was a Morgan Horse with shining, dark brown hair that curled at points. Its eyes were large, black and smart. It strutted elegantly in the confines of the horse stall. I rubbed the back of its neck to introduce myself, as I had been taught to do as a boy. The mare warmed to me. Logan watched Jean and me from the main stable door.

The doomed mare had been relegated to a stall apart from the other horses. This horse was a beautiful Morgan too, but it lay awkwardly on the floor of the stall, and it raised its head to whinny at us when we entered. Noreen told us at dinner that the horse had kicked a farrier, and then a week later it had fallen and twisted a leg when she had taken it riding through the woods. There were hilly woods of brush behind the house. She'd wanted to keep the mare for breeding, but after two failed attempts to breed it, she'd decided to put it down. The horse was angry at us for coming, but it became timid as we retreated.

"It's terrible being all alone here," Noreen said at dinner.

We were sat at table with Logan, as Noreen thought him the only member of her staff that was presentable. She told us so before he came in. He had a longish face with high cheekbones and deep-set brown eyes. He wore his flannel and jeans tightish in cowboy fashion. The heels of his snip-toed boots had been loud on the hardwood floor when he walked in. He was perhaps twenty-four or twenty-five and gave the impression of being strong. He might have been 160 pounds.

"What's so terrible about it?" I asked between bites of the steak. "Being all alone in this big house?"

"Simply being alone is terrible," said Noreen. "Running a business alone as a woman with no family. You couldn't possibly understand. It's terrible."

I wanted to ask her what she would do since it was all so terrible, but I thought it rude to ask. But she said: "I'll go to Mexico or France. I'll have to sell everything. Even the few horses I have left here. I'd rather not sell because to me they're like my children."

Jean reached for my hand under the table.

"But I know you have to be back at the ranch," Noreen said. "Miss Bouverie won't be pleased at you staying the night, but there's no reason to worry over that. I'll call her tonight. I'll tell her there was some issue and you needed to stay here for the night. You'll help me with that matter I need in the morning. No need to do it tonight."

Logan, who had been sitting lightly in his chair, got up. He walked to the door to the dining room, without excusing himself, but before he walked through, he turned around and said: "If you won't be needing me, Ma'am, I'll be getting back to the stable."

"Yes, that's fine," Noreen said.

She raised her glass of water and sipped. Outside, the older stable hand was leading the remaining horses away from the fenced-off grazing land. Noreen excused herself after that. She'd barely touched her steak, but she'd had enough. She didn't eat much, like Miss Bouverie. We heard Noreen's feet patter up the stairs, but they were softer than they should have been. What mine or Jean's would have been. Jean and I returned to our rooms after that. She didn't want to talk, and she didn't come into my room that night. At a late hour, I heard a terrible cry, like that of a woman being murdered, and I sat up in the bed. I imagined that I had dreamt it, but then I heard it a second time. This time I knew it was Noreen, and I threw my legs over the side of the bed. I dressed in my pants and ran out into the hall. But then I thought better of it and returned to the bedroom.

In the morning, I got up before Jean and got dressed. On my way out of the house, I passed Noreen who was sitting in the kitchen. She smiled and waved at me from where she sat at the table. I tapped the side of my belt line to check that I hadn't forgotten my Colt. I met Logan at the door to the stables, but I maneuvered around him. "Hey, wait a minute, Kip," he said. He smelled musty, like he had been up working since dawn. I walked the central corridor of the stable to where the doomed mare rested alone, avoided by the other horses. I opened the narrow door to the stall, and the mare raised her head to watch me. She followed me with her large, sad eyes. I noticed then how trim her body was. Her head was perched on proud, muscular shoulders. I reached for the gun in the holster. "Wait," said Logan, who had trailed me in. One of his hands fell on my shoulder, and he spun me around. He punched me hard in the eye, and I fell back onto the floor of the stall. The horse whinnied, frightened. The gun had rattled out of my hand. I could see it shining in a corner near the stall window when I got up. The window had sleek bars like in a prison cell. I reached for the gun and grabbed it. The mare tried to stand but couldn't with her twisted leg. I aimed the gun at the back of the mare's head and fired.

<h1 style="text-align:center">5</h1>

We stopped in town on the way back to the ranch. I saw Kirk sitting in Vita's and I signaled to Jean to pull over. I was driving the horse transport and Jean was in Hunt's pickup. After we'd both stopped, I told Jean I needed to say hello to someone. Kirk told me he had already sold the cattle that he'd bought from the ranch when I spoke to him. Deals like that were easy for him. We talked for a minute. He was happy and talking in his easy way. I told Kirk Jean was with me. He walked to the window and put his face against the glass. Some of the men in the restaurant laughed. Kirk got a good look at Jean. She was sitting in the driver's seat of Huntley's pickup, just glancing out the window at the street. When Kirk saw that pretty girl sitting in that truck, he walked over and gave me a friendly pat on the back.

Jean truly was pretty. We reached the ranch that afternoon. Huntley ran out of the house to me as we walked up the porch steps. He was attired in shorts and thick wool socks. His socks peaked out from the tops of his hobnailed boots. His calves were hairy considering how young he was. He ran out of the house but slowed as he neared us. He told me that Hannah had died. He'd only met her once, but he was sad about it. She'd been found that morning. He said a neighbor had been con-cerned because Hannah hadn't shown up to a date the night before. The neighbor saw her body through the window when he was driving by and had called while Jean and I were away. Huntley hugged me because that's what grieving people do.

Jean didn't know about Hannah. We'd been separated for a while, but we hadn't divorced as Hannah had told me she knew too many couples who divorced only to marry one another again later. She'd thought we were the type of people that would do that. We'd met twelve years ago when we were both very young and desperate to be married, as some people are. Jean said she was sorry, and her footsteps were mournful as she walked away to Miss Bouverie's house. I heard her footsteps patter on the hardwood floor in that house. I heard when she ran into Babette, and I tried to listen to their whispered speech. I couldn't make it out. I heard the shutting of Jean's bedroom door.

The next morning, Babette told me that Miss Bouverie wanted to see me. There was a cattle smell in the air. That persistent cattle smell. When I met the lady, she asked me how things had gone and where the mare was. I told her. Miss Bouverie didn't know anything about the trip yet because we hadn't seen her. Miss Bouverie asked me to shut the door. I shut the door behind me. I could hear Babette's footsteps in the hall. Miss Bouverie wanted to know about Jean: if we had slept together and if Jean was a virgin. She asked me about the clothes that Jean had worn, like someone would want to know what the condemned person had worn before they'd been electrocuted. Someone who never leaves the house. I told her that Jean had worn a pretty dress to see Noreen.

"Someone will have to drive the horse transport back to Noreen's," I said.

"I don't want to talk about that. I'm tired," said Miss Bouverie. She smoothed the soft tresses of her hair.

"Yes, Miss. I just wanted to know who was going."

Miss Bouverie tried to sit up in bed. I reached forward to help her, but she smacked my hand away.

"Fine, you can go," she said. "I don't mean to be rough. I'm not feeling well. You know how I am. One day I'm well and then bang."

She forced a smile. She said: "You can go tomorrow, if you'd like."

"Yes, Miss. That's when I'll go."

I turned and began to walk from the room. I saw the legs of the toy horse still peeking from under the bed.

When I reached the porch, I saw a veterinary technician coming up the porch steps. He put the empty bucket he was carrying down and greeted me with his dirty hands. He shook my hands, and I got the dirt from his own onto mine. I didn't even know what the dirt was from. Then Huntley came out of the house, looking expectantly at me. I told him that I'd help him with the cattle tomorrow, but then I had to drive back to Thibault County. I didn't need his truck since I was just driving the horse transport back to where I'd gotten it from. "When are you gonna get your own truck?" he asked. From the lowest porch step, we watched the cattle doctors standing about twenty yards off. Talking. We couldn't make out their words because they were too far away.

When I reached Noreen's house in Thibault County, I didn't find the lady waiting for me on the steps as I had before. I found the two stable hands instead. There was Logan and the elderly man whose name I never learned. Logan walked away as I neared the door, but the elderly man took two steps toward me. "Be careful with her," he said. I knocked on the house door when I reached it. Noreen didn't come to the door but yelled: "Come in!" The door was unlocked. I pushed it and it swung with a loud creak. I found Noreen in the part of the hall nearest the kitchen. I was surprised to find Noreen attired in a frilly dress and Mary Janes like Jean had worn at dinner. Noreen had also dyed her dark hair the same shade of auburn as Jean's. Her face was painted in an unnatural way. "I thought you'd like to come in for a cup of coffee," she said. "I'm making it myself since Gladys has the day off. And you can spend the night hear with me if you want."

"I just need to drop off the truck, Ma'am," I told Noreen. "I hope it's all right if I leave it out front. I just pulled up on the front lawn."

"Why are your forearms that way? All veiny?" Noreen asked. "Is that because you're working outside all day?"

"That's part of it. Where did you want me to leave the transport?"

"Out front is fine," said Noreen. She allowed one of her hands to fall on my forearm. She traced the length of a vein with a long, white finger. "Come this way," she said, pulling me along behind her by the arm.

We went into the kitchen where steam was hissing from the coffeemaker. The whole space smelled like coffee.

"I called Odette before you came so she won't be mad if you spend some time here. It's all right."

Noreen's face was like a mask. You didn't know what the person beneath looked like and you didn't know if the person beneath was kind.

"I was just thinking you don't know anything about me," Noreen went on. "There isn't much to know. My sister and I inherited this farm after our parents died. 25,000 acres. Then my sister died and I inherited it myself. I was living in New York at the time. In Staten Island, if you can believe that. I had met a man and was living with him. He was of the Mediterranean type, very physical and old-fashioned, and I was absolutely addicted. Addicted is a strong word, but that's what I was. He worked out a lot and was all muscley. You remind me of him actually. Anyway, I came back here when my sister got sick. I never went back to New York. Then when my sister passed, I took over the place. There's the horse farm, but we grow feed too. And other things. It's too ridiculous to talk about. It's only been a few years since I've been running this place. I'm not as old as you might think."

"I don't think you're old, Ma'am."

"No, I'm not old. Sometimes you feel like you're getting old when you're living alone in the country. Like the world is passing you by or you don't know what other people are doing. You don't know how to relate to them or if you still can at all."

We were sitting now and Noreen had one of her hands atop one of mine. When she saw that I'd finished my coffee, she picked up my coffee cup and refilled it. She made my coffee the way she made her own. Rich with cream. "I never went back to New York, and I never saw my Italian friend again." She laughed. "I've known Odette for 15 years. We went to the University of Texas together. I get the impression you're about our age or a little younger. She's very cryptic."

Noreen passed her long fingers through her dyed hair. It wasn't obvious that it wasn't her natural color. I only knew because I'd seen her hair before she'd dyed it. Noreen continued to talk as if it was an accepted fact that I was spending the night with her, even though I hadn't agreed. I thought it'd be rude to argue. She knew that I would abide. She said something about supper. Then she got up from the table. Her Mary Janes made hardly a sound as she walked away. These were flat shoes unlike the heels she'd worn before. After she left, I noticed the strange things that had been placed in cabinets on the wall. There was a display of honey jars near the door that lead to the bedrooms. Honey jars are often made in the shape of bears since there's an idea that bears love honey. It's their favorite thing in the world if you believe the cartoons. These jars were all in the shape of pot-bellied bears. Some of the bears were made from plastic. The Texas heat had warped their faces. But their insurmountable love of honey was still seen in their eyes. The bears all wore hats like Smokey the Bear.

Logan avoided me when I went out on the rear lawn, but the elderly stable hand approached. There was something in the man's face and demeanor that seemed very old, although he was in good physical shape. He told me that Noreen was a bad person. He told me in the gossipy way that some older people have. As if they believe everything they hear and feel it their duty to inform everyone else. He wasn't a malicious person, just gossipy. I thought it'd be rude to repeat to him some of the things that Noreen had said in the house, so I just listened to the things that he said. He didn't seem to like silence. If I fell silent, he just started talking again. He wore blue jean overalls that were different from the duck overalls that Logan wore. Logan had walked away when I stepped onto the lawn, but he occasionally reappeared. He had a rake in his hand and pretended like he was raking the leaves piled up near the stable door. But they had already been raked. They were set neatly in a pile about five feet tall.

I heard the whinnies of the horses that hadn't been let out. The elderly man asked me to help him wash the stall where the mare I'd shot had been. He brought the hose, and I held it when he went back to turn it on.

When I went back to the house, I found Noreen in the hall. She was wearing a sheer dress, like a negligee. I saw how red her hair was, and how the gauze of the negligee set it off. Her hair was not a burning red, but a soft red like Jean's hemophiliac blood. Jean had told me on the drive back to Miss Bouverie's that her parents had given her up because they couldn't take care of her. After years in foster care, she was adopted by a woman who was actually her father's first wife. By then, her parents had died.

After watching me for a few moments, Noreen ran into my arms. I felt the heft of her bosom against my chest. Her areolas were large and knobby and I felt them through my shirt. I was wearing a thin flannel shirt. It was thin because I'd had it for at least two years and had washed it by hand many times.

In bed, Noreen told me that the variety of lilac she had in her garden was called Mrs. Edward Harding. She was obsessed with candles. She asked me if she could take one of the candles she had lit in the hall and pour the wax on my body. She giggled like a schoolgirl when she said it. She told me I had a beautiful body. She wanted to see the wax dry against my muscles. She wanted to see my body twitch when the hot wax touched my skin. I told her no, and I turned away from her in the bed to show that I meant it. But then I still felt her hungry hands all over me.

I ran into the elderly man again the next day. I saw Logan too. He was sitting in a truck, but he didn't say anything. I realized that I stupidly hadn't thought about how I would get back home. The transport was brought back, but now I didn't have a ride. The elderly man said that I shouldn't believe all the stories that Noreen was filling my head with.

"She told me she came back here when her sister got sick and then she inherited the place when she died," I said.

The old man laughed. He said: "I've been here 20 years. She never had any sister. She was an only child."

He said that people fell prey to her because she was rich and reasonably attractive. That's what he called her. Reasonably attractive. At that point, I realized that I would have to get a ride back to Miss Bouverie's from Logan. That's why Logan was sitting angrily in the truck like that. He didn't want to drive me. Before I got into the truck, Noreen came out. One of her hands was made mysteriously into a fist. I walked toward her. When I reached her, she opened her fist to reveal several $100 bills. She looked around to ensure no one saw us. Then she shoved the money into my hands like I was a common whore. I drove off with Logan in his old Ford truck. He didn't say a word to me the whole way.

I joined Huntley in the fields when I got back. I didn't stop at the house to let Mrs. Bouverie know that I'd returned. Huntley was quiet as if he could smell Noreen on me. He didn't keep off. He just didn't say anything. When we were done for the day and going back to the house, he told me that Jean had left the ranch. I was surprised and stared at him. He said it wasn't a big deal. Miss Bouverie had told her the day before she could go back to her house to pick up clothes and things. Her sister had come to pick her up.

"But she hasn't come back?" I asked Huntley.

"No," he answered.

"Is she gone for good?"

"Not that I know of."

"Don't lie, Hunt."

"I'm not. She's coming back. She just went to town to get some things."

"Then why isn't she back yet?"

"I don't know," said Huntley.

Huntley sighed as he handed me the keys to his pickup.

I told him that I'd be a minute since I wanted to inject first. I told him it didn't feel right that I hadn't injected yesterday. I thought I'd take both equipoise and winstrol. Winstrol comes in an oral form, but the compound I take is a liquid injectable.

I went straight to Jean's window when I reached her house since I didn't want to meet her sister again. I had to jump to tap on her window, even though she lived on the first floor. The house was sat high up off the ground. She came to the window in her negligee. She smiled when she saw me. She opened the window for me to come in. Jean was beautiful in her negligee, bra and panties, and her auburn hair was pulled back. This made the startling bone structure of her face more prominent than it typically was. She asked if I could lay in bed with her for a few minutes. The bed made a soft creak as Jean and I got into it.

"Ain't we goin' back?" I asked her.

"I don't know."

"Fine," I said.

"I won't take advantage," I told her some minutes later.

"It's fine. I don't care," Jean said.

We lay like that for a time. Then it started to get dark and I decided I should head back. Jean had moved to a sitting position on the edge of the bed. "I saw Miss Bouverie," she said. I tried to hide my alarm, but then I laughed.

"You don't mean you saw her here?" I asked through chuckles.

"Yes, I do."

"You couldn't have."

"Why couldn't I have?"

"Because Miss Bouverie is on the other side of town and she can't walk."

"How do you know she can't walk?" said Jean. "I saw her. I got up early this morning and went outside to walk on the grass. I saw her driving by in her car."

"What kind of car was it?"

"It was a Ford."

"Jean, Miss Bouverie has a wasting disease. She's dying slowly and she can't walk."

"So you think she has the same thing the cattle have," Jean said.

"I don't know. How would I know?"

"You don't know anything, do you?"

"Jean, stop."

I told Jean to get dressed. Miss Bouverie wouldn't be happy she'd been gone so long. The best thing to do would be for her to get dressed and we'd both go back. "But what if she tries to come into my room?" Jean asked. I told her she was being ridiculous. I asked her why Miss Bouverie would want to come into her bedroom, even if she could. "Maybe she wants to hurt me," Jean said. I watched her get dressed. She decided on a pair of jeans, and after she'd taken off the negligee, she pulled the jeans over her legs. She was so slight that the pants came right on without a hitch. I noticed she had a bruise on her arm when she was buttoning up her blouse.

"What happened to your arm?"

"No, it's nothing. We won't even talk about it," she said.

"But what happened?"

"Don't talk to me like that, please. I'm not a child."

"Jean, you have hemophilia."

"I know I have hemophilia. It's nothing. These things happen. These small bruises pop up and they go away after a week or so. It's annoying but I've learned not to be bothered by them. I've lived with this for a long time. Why don't we go? I'm dressed. You wanted me to go back, didn't you?"

We left Jean's sister's house the same way I'd come in. We went out through the window. We both giggled like schoolchildren. I saw Jean's sister sitting in the front room when I reached the truck. She didn't say anything, and she turned away when she noticed me looking at her. I opened the door for Jean and said: "Hold on a minute." I scooped her up by the legs and carried her the few remaining steps to the truck's passenger side door. I set her down in the passenger seat as best as I could. "Because of the bruise," I told her, and she laughed.

6

Supper was served late that night. I sensed something strange in the air as soon as we reached the ranch because there were men that I hadn't seen before gathered by the stables. The stables were far away from the house, but you could see them on the approach. There was a new horse transport and two men. The men wore chaps and cowboy hats. One of them turned to watch me as I drove to the house with Jean. He spit his chewing tobacco out onto the ground as men do.

We heard the laughter of an unfamiliar woman in Miss Bouverie's house. Huntley told us that there was a guest that would be staying at the house for a few days. He was standing out front. "What are you talking about?" I asked, even though I suspected it was true. It was just like Miss Bouverie to surprise you. To pull out the rug from under you. The woman was sitting in the living room, and Babette was talking to her freely as if she herself weren't a servant. For her part, the woman did the same: chatting freely with Babette like old friends. The woman turned toward Jean and me when she saw us in the hall.

That's when Babette said: "Oh, Kip, you're back. We're having a late supper tonight. There's a guest."

"Just call me Chantal," said the woman. Babette blocked her from our view so I couldn't see her well.

Babette told us that we would be having dinner with her. Of course, Miss Bouverie wouldn't be joining us as she never left the upstairs. When Babette had done speaking, Jean walked toward the stairs with slow, childish steps. I asked her what was wrong. I was wondering if it had anything to do with her illness, but she said that it didn't. I didn't need to change. So I went into the powder room to wash my hands and splash water on my face. The powder room. That's what the women called it. I wanted to inject myself with the horse steroids but I didn't have any syringes on me.

We were already all gathered in the dining room by the time Jean came down. The dining room was seldom used since Miss Bouverie never came down to eat in it. There was no reason for the servants to use the dining room without her. That's essentially what we were. We were her servants. Chantal was immediately chatty. She wasn't as predatory as Noreen. Not right away. She asked Jean to take the seat beside her. Chantal sat at the head of the table as the representative of Miss Bouverie, since she was her friend. I found myself in the position of sitting at the foot of the table, directly across from Chantal.

"It's nice to be in the country again," Chantal said after we had mostly finished our meal. Babette cooked the venison we ate. A stuffed buck head regarded us suspiciously from its place on the wall.

"Is it nice, Ma'am?" Huntley asked politely.

"Oh yes, it is," said Chantal. "Even the manners of the people I find quite nice. I'm a big city girl, if you couldn't tell. I won't tell you which city. Let's just say that I've lived all over the world. I've lived in cities all over, including here. In the States."

Chantal was a tall, shapely woman with platinum blond hair. She had a European accent, but she told us she'd lived in the States for some time. I hadn't met anyone like her before.

"So you're just visiting then?" Huntley asked. "If you don't mind me asking."

"Huntley," Babette said, with a laugh.

"No, I actually bought a property nearby," Chantal said. "But I'm not often there. I just got back from Houston. I've been doing some renovating, traveling around. You know how it is. I promised Odette I would spend a few days with her since she doesn't go out. I've been meaning to meet all of you."

I didn't say anything to that, but Huntley said: "Have you been meaning to, Ma'am?"

"I have," said Chantal. "And, of course, you noticed the buckskin horses that I brought with me. I had my boys come along with me. My workers, I mean. Miss Bouverie didn't ask for buckskins, she has no need for them, but I brought them anyway. At least she can keep them for a while, and if she doesn't like them, she can give them back to me. Buckskin is just a color of a horse as you know. Buckskin-colored horses. I know she has the working horses and that Morgan mare that she recently got. It's so nice to have horses around."

"We also get wild horses around here, Ma'am," said Huntley. "Feral."

"Yes, it's nice. I had been meaning to pay a visit."

Then Chantal turned to Jean beside her. I sat up higher in my chair. Jean looked so frail beside Chantal. Chantal was sort of a muscular woman. Her defined shoulders were like sensuous slabs of meat in her spaghetti-strap blouse. Jean's hair was still pulled back from her face. It seemed to me that she was bracing herself.

"And Gail, you're so pretty," Chantal said and smiled.

"It's Jean," I said.

"That's right. Jean," said Chantal. "It's a masculine name. Is that short for something?"

"No, it isn't," said Jean.

"Oh, I see," said Chantal. "You came up on the phone the other day because there were some questions about you. Such a pretty girl. I suppose someone had seen you somewhere. You might have been in a film. Well, films actually. Plural. Does that sound familiar?"

"Ma'am?" Jean asked.

Although we were mostly done eating, Huntley wasn't, and his utensils made a happy clang against his plate.

"You were featured in some small-scale productions, I've heard," Chantal said. "Films if we can call them that. I suppose it's brave that someone in your condition would star in movies. It could be dangerous for you. You could get hurt. I heard you starred in a production called *How To Be Pretty*. It was a direct-to-video release, as I understand it."

Jean played with her spoon in the bowl. She said: "I don't see what that has to do with anything."

"Oh, it does, sweetie," said Chantal. "It has everything to do with it," and Chantal laughed in a mean kind of way. "It has to do with a lot of things. It was a horror film. You were frolicking with young men on a beach in Florida or Alabama somewhere. Getting up to all sorts of naughty things."

Babette, who had been sitting with us, got up from the table and began to clear it as we were mostly finished.

"It was a low-budget film," said Jean.

"It was a low-budget film," echoed Chantal. "And did you display your breasts in that film?"

Jean chuckled. "Did I display my breasts? Do you mean was I topless?"

"Yes, that's what I mean."

"If you must know, I did display my breasts, as you so nicely put it. It was a horror movie. The young women often are topless in those. It wasn't anything indecent."

"Oh, I'm sure it wasn't anything indecent. I'm sure Mom and Pop were pleased."

"That's not a very nice thing to say," said Huntley, unhappy and disappointed like a child.

"Oh, no, of course I didn't mean it like how you're thinking about it," said Chantal. "It's just seeing your daughter in a film, that must be interesting. I imagine it must be. I'm sure they didn't think it was indecent seeing some hairy man groping their daughter and then killing her."

"They wouldn't have seen that hairy man as they were already dead," said Jean. "They'd been dead for years. I was in and out of the hospital as a child. I was in foster care. There wasn't anyone to chastise me or be disappointed."

"You see, I've seen the film," said Chantal. "As you said, it was a horror film. We were just curious, that's all. The girl in the film was pretty. She had a narrow, girlish waist. Small hands. She wore these summery clothes. Halter tops and swaying skirts. Mary Janes. They styled her hair so nicely, the production team. They must have really liked her since they styled her better than anyone else. I didn't know it was you as I had never met you before. Now I know it was you. But that was a long time ago. What, about three years?"

I didn't see much of Chantal after that. I spent several days isolating myself in the fields with Hunt and the cattle. Then Friday rolled around, and I'd already told Miss Bouverie that I'd be out because of Hannah's funeral. Her neighbors had arranged it. All I had to do was show. When I got back, I joined up with Hunt and the cattle. I felt out of sorts as I'd spent so much time away from them. There was a quality the cattle had that was better than people. I helped Hunt to calf them when it was time. I had more experience than he did as I was ten years older and had been around livestock most of that time, but I let him do it. Huntley was happy like a kid seeing the newborn calves in the pens with the heifers. His giddiness rubbed off on me at times. The calves liked to have you pet them. They liked when you scratched the back of their necks when they realized that you were the sort that would do that. But I had been away from it for a time.

When I reached Hunt, he told me that I should go back to the house. Chantal was waiting for me. "What for?" I asked him, and he told me that the lady wanted a ride into town. Her workers had gone back to her ranch, and she didn't have a vehicle here. I pointed out to Hunt that he was the one with the free pickup, and he said: "But she wants you to drive her." I didn't go to her immediately. I was feeling low so I went into the house and up to my room to inject myself. Equipoise and winstrol. Winstrol is an anabolic steroid that was first released in 1962. The generic name is Stanozolol. It's prohibited in most professional sports, but it's still commonly given to horses to improve performance. It used to be indicated in some medical conditions like dwarfism but became prohibited after human growth hormone became common. I didn't have Jean to inject me in the backside, so I did it myself. I was standing in front of the mirror in my room. I was looking really good. The mirror wasn't full-length. It only went up to my waist, but I could see enough of myself to see the needle tip push into my muscle. The buttock didn't hurt as much as the shoulder. Even if a man is fairly lean, he still has more fat in his buttock than in his shoulder, most likely because of the high concentration of androgen receptors in the shoulders. It was nice to have a girl inject you when she hasn't done it before because you can see the thrill and wonder in her eyes.

Chantal was already sitting in Huntley's pickup when I made it down to the driveway. She watched me in the rearview mirror as I approached. I brought an unopened box of winstrol for Kirk since he told me he wanted to try it. He already had syringes. I knew he wouldn't inject, but I figured I'd give it to him anyway since he was paying for it. He was paying more than what I'd paid. Chantal politely didn't say anything when I put the box of steroids in the back seat. She smiled expectantly at me as if she wanted to say something. The truck had a tight back seat as some trucks have.

Chantal squealed in delight when we passed a team of wild horses on the road. It didn't surprise me that we saw them. Hunt had mentioned them when we had dinner with Chantal. It was as if he willed them into existence. The dust cloud from their feet was still with us when we reached the railroad crossing. The way into town we took involved driving over the tracks since Chantal had to go the pharmacy. It was quicker to reach the pharmacy this way. I thought I'd make it across without a hitch, but about six feet away from the raised barrier, the alarm sounded. I brought the truck to a sudden stop and Chantal jolted forward prettily. We both laughed. We waited impatiently for the barrier to lower and then for the train to roll across. The train rumbled loudly across the tornado-scarred land. Near the train tracks was a cracked oak that a man had tried and failed to chop down. The boughs leaned partially over the tracks, and he'd left the ax in the trunk of the tree.

In the parking lot of the pharmacist's, Chantal made small talk. She said that there was always a line at the pharmacist's, and she didn't like waiting in line with other people. Chantal scooted toward the door to leave the truck, but before she did, she turned to me. She told me she hoped I didn't think she was mean for talking to Jean like she did. She said that there were questions about Jean and she had to ask. She didn't say who had the questions. It seemed absurd to me that anyone would have a problem with Jean. No one had a problem with the fawns you passed on the road. You just drove past them. Then she asked about Hannah. I told her it was true that I had been married to her and she'd recently died. I was the heir of her estate as her husband, but because she had cousins who were making trouble all I was coming into for the time being was the house. Everything else she had was tied up in probate.

I saw Chantal's agile body coming out of the pharmacist's when she was done. She was agile like a filly. She asked me if I'd drive her back to her place. She wasn't leaving Miss Bouverie's for good. She just wanted to get a bathing suit since the weather had been so nice. It didn't seem nice of her to sunbathe when Miss Bouverie was an invalid who couldn't do any of that, but it wasn't my place to say so. She didn't have to come to the Bouverie ranch to sunbathe. She had her own place.

"I'm hiring another hand on the ranch," she said as we neared the railroad crossing. We had to cross it to get to her place too.

"Really."

"Yes, I have so many horses and it seems like too much for the three guys I have. Maybe I'll just get a trainer. There's actually someone in town. Do you know Nathan?"

"I think I do."

"Yes, he said he knew you," said Chantal. "I raise thorough-breds. I don't know if you knew that."

"Is that why you're getting rid of your buckskins? Because you only want bay thoroughbreds?" I asked her. I only said it because I felt I had to say something.

"No, I don't mind buckskin thoroughbreds," Chantal said. "I actually like that color. I used to have buckskin ponies when I was a girl, but then my father had to sell the farm."

I wondered why she asked me if I knew Nathan if she'd already heard that he knew me.

"I don't understand why my cattle and horses are fine and hers are dying. Even she's dying," said Chantal.

"I don't know what you mean."

"I mean about Odette," said Chantal. "I don't understand why it's just her place."

"I don't understand it either," I said.

"You could come in for a second when we get to my house," Chantal said. "If you want."

"No, I'd better not."

"Just for a minute."

The driveway to Chantal's house had been paved with new paving stones recently, she told me. This set it apart from Miss Bouverie's ranch where nothing was new. It seemed as if Chantal had spent a large sum of money on the place since she'd bought it. Miss Bouverie had inherited her family ranch, but Chantal's ranch had been bought by the lady herself. I didn't know how she made her money. She was swimming in it. I think she was the only person I met who I could say that about. Although Miss Bouverie's house didn't give the impression that a rich person lived there and it was almost one hundred years old, it was a home. Chantal's house didn't seem like a home. Inside, the house was filled with material things and many mirrors. The mirrors reflected the wood paneling and the bay horses grazing outside. All the horses I saw were bays even though Chantal said that she didn't have a preference for bays. She poured me a glass of wine even though I had to drive back to the Bouverie ranch. It was only ten miles away, but I still had to drive. She was already a different person after one drink, and that's when I realized she was an alcoholic. It seemed strange to me that Miss Bouverie would be friends with someone like her, but I suppose they weren't really friends. Chantal was coming on to me by the second drink. She was touching me in a forceful, unfriendly way. She pushed her fingers through the gaps in my shirt at one point: the sideways gaps made by the buttons. I pushed her away roughly. That infuriated her. I didn't mean to push her so hard, but I was strong since I was injecting veterinary steroids all the time. She said: "Why did you come here then? What the heck is wrong with you?" I thought it was rude of her to think I owed her sex just because I stepped inside for a minute. Some people didn't understand basic politeness anymore. Manners. I turned to walk out, and she stumbled and fell to her knees.

"I'll call her," Chantal said, as if I had been the one that made her fall. "I'll call Odette. That's exactly what I'll do. I'll call her and you'll be looking for another job, mister!"

She seemed to take great satisfaction in that last mister. It was all so ridiculous since I knew she wasn't attracted to me. She was just lonely: a lonely, rich woman living on a ranch with a fully-stocked wine cellar and no man. I was just a physical body to her. She wanted a man with a sleek, agile body like the bay horses outside.

I met Jean in Miss Bouverie's house. She reminded me that we'd promised to have dinner with Babette at her place. Babette had a place of her own. As Jean and I walked through the fields to get there, I saw the way Jean looked back at the house with new choler. It wasn't like Jean to show she was upset. When horses were irritable, we said they had choler. I had grown up around horses, but my family had to sell the farm and we moved away. But my oldest memories were of the horses tumbling over the head of the plain as I watched them from the rear windows of the house.

Babette's house was an RV parked on a back field of the Bouverie ranch. Babette had money of her own, but she was saving up to become a rancher herself. Serving as a cook for Miss Bouverie was an easy way for her to earn money. Or so she told Jean and me at dinner. She was happy and smiling when she met us at the door to the RV. Her hair was down, and she looked younger. The RV was more spacious than it looked from the outside. More spacious than RVs usually were. The walls had been fashioned in that kind of plastic board that looks like wood. The windows were open. The windows let in fresh air and the cattle smell. "The ranch hands are getting younger and younger," Babette said, but I knew she wasn't talking about me. She was referring to Huntley, who was basically new. Jean and

I followed Babette to the dining area of the RV. Babette told us she'd be back in a moment after we'd sat down.

"I thought we'd have coffee first," she said. "Then we'll eat. I won't make you sing for your supper."

"Good, 'cause I can't," I told her.

"Of course, you can," Babette said. "You sang a James Taylor song at a competition. Yes, I heard about that."

"You didn't," said Jean, grinning from ear to ear.

"He did," said Babette.

Babette trotted off to the kitchenette after that. Jean didn't speak, though she was seated next to me. I could tell she was mad about the things Chantal had said to her. Later, I would tell Babette and Jean that Chantal was a drunk, but I didn't tell them what else had happened at her house. When they asked me how I knew, I just shook my head. From where we were, I could see how the road snaked in the direction of Chantal's property. But you couldn't see the road because of the tall, dry grass. You had to know it was there. I knew. The wind blew grass from far off against the window. We both turned our heads eagerly towards Babette when she returned with a thermos and two Styrofoam cups. Jean said it was nice this way. She said it was like we were at a picnic.

"Miss Bouverie's bringing more horses on," I said.

"She should since she's getting better," said Babette.

She poured the first Styrofoam cup of coffee.

"No, she isn't," I said.

Jean was ill at ease, which she displayed by sitting up higher in her seat. But she smiled good-naturedly at us. I thought it was part of her illness, to always try to appear as if she were well. Outside, a calf settled in the shade of Babette's RV. I wondered how it had gotten all the way down here.

"Well, buying horses won't make up for what's happening to the cattle," said Babette.

"I agree."

I could hear the sizzle of whatever Babette was cooking in the kitchenette rolling from behind us.

"Hopefully Chantal won't come around again," said Babette.

"Babette!" cried Jean.

"I mean it," Babette said. "Before she bought her own place, she used to come here to sunbathe. She would lie in front of the house with her big, floppy breasts. Trying to get everyone to look at her. Don't get me wrong, she has nice breasts. I just think the whole package is too much, you know what I mean? And why come here to do that?"

"Oh, she'll be sunbathing again this year," I said.

"See what I mean? She's just such a shameless person. I don't even know how she knows Miss Bouverie."

"Rich people always know all kinds of people," I said.

"That's true," said Babette. "Chantal used to live in California. I think Miss Bouverie would go to California with Chantal if she was well. In fact, I think she would sell the ranch and go to California with Chantal if she could."

"No, she wouldn't," I said. "She might travel, but she wouldn't sell the ranch."

"Perhaps not," said Babette. "She wouldn't terminate us. She wouldn't terminate Huntley."

I'd briefly seen Huntley when I made it back to the house from Chantal's. Huntley's mustache was coming in. He looked like a character from a movie with his curly blond hair and dark blond mustache. Always dressed in tight blue jeans. Huntley never cast any mercenary looks at anyone because he didn't have it in him. Before I met Jean, Huntley had told me about how he'd gone away to college for a year but left because he'd felt out of place there. Dumb and out of place. He failed a math test and that was it. He was injecting with steroids too at one time, but he'd stopped. As we sat there, Huntley was only twenty years old.

"Were you talking about Huntley when you said that the ranch hands were getting younger and younger?" I asked Babette.

"Of course," laughed Babette. "Tell her about Trey."

"Trey?" asked Jean.

"No, you tell her," I said, shaking my head.

"Well, there was a guy who worked here late last year named Trey," Babette began. "Dumb as can be."

"That's not fair," I said.

"Well, it's true. He was big and dumb, and Miss Bouvier had to get rid of him after only a couple months. But I knew you were friends with him."

Babette glanced at me after she said it. It was true. Trey wasn't the brightest, but he was harmless. He practically ate Miss Bouverie out of house and home. It wasn't hard to understand as he was the most massive human I'd seen up front. He looked like his father had been shooting him in the ass with human growth hormone since he was 14.

We didn't stay the whole night at Babette's. Babette put some old records on, and we laughed and drank wine. Babette didn't have a TV. The light bulbs in her RV never got very bright. The lighting in the place set off Babette's kind of prettiness. Her looks were dark and simmering. Dark hair. Dark eyes. I thought she was pretty, but there was something brazen about her, and I found it hard to be attracted to her. I found her similar to Chantal. I didn't know how Jean felt. She laughed and had a good time in Babette's RV, but never seemed herself. As the women looked through one of Babette's old photo albums, I sat in a chair with my legs spread wide apart. I missed the riding that I used to do when I was young. Riding correct, expensive horses wasn't the same as riding the working horses that Miss Bouverie kept on the ranch for Huntley and me. There was something elegant about an expensive horse. I thought it'd be nice to have horses of my own. I'd buy racehorses, so I could go to the high-stakes races and talk with the other racing men who owned racehorses and bet on them. I'd be like Kirk, who made friends with men of his own ilk. Kirk had made friends with the cattlemen, and that was why he was doing so well. I'd have cattle too and recreate the same life I'd had here. Roping, branding, castrating.

Soon Babette was drunk, and we left her there in the RV in the wee hours of the morning. We saw a light on in Miss Bouverie's bedroom as we neared the house. I told Jean we should stop in the stables. We watched the horses from above the stall doors though we didn't wake them. A disturbed horse might kick you. It was clear that Miss Bouverie's family had once bred horses since there were stalls for dozens of them. The stable building was as wide as the house. I knew it was only a matter of time before Miss Bouverie acquired more horses. Especially if she got better. I'd have to get a hose in there and wash the stalls out to make readiness for them.

7

I knew Miss Bouverie would suggest I go back to Noreen's. It was late morning when I heard from Babette that the lady wanted me. I was already on the land with Hunt. I went with Babette to the house, and she closed the door softly behind me after I walked into Miss Bouverie's bedroom. The Colt rattled on the bedside table when Miss Bouverie tried to sit up. The bed had wobbled and struck the table. Miss Bouverie was displeased with the dirt on my chaps, but she didn't say so. She only gave me a particular look. But she smiled sweetly thereafter. She said: "You wouldn't have heard because you're up so early, but Jean is gone. She took her things and left." I paced the room. I took off my hat and swatted at the air. I told Miss Bouverie that she was wrong. She had to be. It wasn't like Jean to do things without telling anyone. I'd been with her only last night. "But you don't really know her," said Miss Bouverie. She was right. She said there wasn't any need searching the property because it'd already been done. I suggested walking down to the stables to check. That's when Miss Bouverie suggested I go to Noreen's.

"Thibault County is nearly three hours away, Miss," I said.

"You might come across Jean on the road."

"You don't have that correct, Miss," I told her. "Jean wouldn't go that way."

"I'm not looking to argue. Look, I'm tired. There's something here that's making me sick. Maybe it's the ground water."

Miss Bouverie didn't drink the ground water. I reminded her of that. Hunt or I had to go to town to get boxes of bottled water every two weeks. Miss Bouverie looked at me like I was something on the bottom of her foot or the toy horse under the bed. "But the ground water gets into everything," she said. She shifted in her bed. She smoothed a crinkle in the ruffled collar of her dress.

"Babette cooks with it. She cleans. It's in the rag that she cleans with. That's what I was meaning to say. Noreen is having a get-together tonight. I just need you to stop by. And make sure to change before you go. Look for Jean on the road, check the motels and gas stations on the way, and then pop in to say good evening to Noreen. Go change. You can wear your jeans, but at least put on a clean shirt. Don't look at me that way. I don't know why you're angry. You know how I feel. When I'm better, we'll go someplace far away. Now go put on a clean shirt."

I washed my clothes by hand. Miss Bouverie knew that. I had done it since I'd managed a ranch for a year after college. There I had been the only person tending the herd, and there wasn't any washing machine. And when I hung my clothes on the lines behind the house, I could see Miss Bouverie watching me from the window. Behind me, the pumpjacks and the grain elevators.

I passed teams of grain elevators when I entered Thibault County. Thibault County was a closed farming community. Everyone knew everyone else and the air in the county was biting in winter. It wasn't winter yet. The women were up for anything. That's what Hunt told me. He said you started to see them in the wintertime in their suede jackets. Thibault had been named for a soldier that had fought in the Texan independence war, but sometimes people thought it was named after Jocelyn Thibault who played for the Montreal Canadiens. It was an absolutely ridiculous thing to hear. Jocelyn Thibault hadn't even been born when this land was named Thibault. Hunt was one of those who believed Thibault County was named for Jocelyn Thibault, who played goaltender for the Canadiens.

The railroad line ran right through Noreen's property. It connected to the Santa Fe railroad. Behind that, the village Noreen called a town. I thought the rail line was abandoned as it had grass growing between the planks and weeds tumbling over the irons, but I heard the freight train carrying grain when I left the place the next morning. Noreen wouldn't have noticed the sound as she was the owner of a large property. 25,000 acres, as she said. She lived far away from the trains even if they ran through her land. When I found her, it was growing dark as I'd spent most of the day stopping off at places searching for Jean. At motels and gas stations as Miss Bouverie wanted. It wasn't Noreen who opened the door. It was a hand that I hadn't met before. "Oh, that's Mino," said Noreen after I greeted her and asked who it was. There were already men gathered in the open spaces inside the house. The dining room, the kitchen, and the parlor. There were few women. Soon after Noreen started speaking, a man bumped into a table and a lamp fell off and shattered on the floor. The men all laughed. It was the deep, hearty laughter of cattlemen.

Mino stood beside me at the door for a minute, but then he raised his hat and bowed a little. He turned his back to the party and went outside. The inside of Noreen's house was like a large farmhouse or two farmhouses tacked together. The walls were thin, but that left more space for inside the rooms. The men were outdoor folk: cattlemen like those Kirk did business with. After Noreen led me into the house, she disappeared into a circle of men standing in the parlor. Originally on the outskirts, she was soon practically in the center of the circle as they chatted happily about one thing or another. I reckoned she liked to be at the center of things. I moved off to a man wearing a rawhide jacket who was sipping something clear in a glass by the back window of the house. I didn't want to speak to him. I just thought it was strange standing alone. But the man said: "She's comely, isn't she?" I presumed he was speaking about Noreen. I agreed, though I didn't feel strongly inclined to agree. Comely seemed like an old-fashioned thing to say about someone.

When I walked out of the house through the kitchen door, I heard the loud chatter of the people rolling behind me until it suddenly stopped when the door shut. I was only outside for a minute or so when Noreen appeared behind me. She approached me, and her feet made a crunching sound on the grass. The ominous sound of Noreen's feet on the grass always remained with me even after Miss Bouverie killed her. The grass was artificially green like AstroTurf.

"Mino was brought on after Logan left," Noreen remarked.

"I didn't know that Logan left," I said.

"It was only a few days ago," said Noreen. "I think he didn't like all the men who used to come to see me. You know, I'm a businesswoman so obviously there'll be men over. He didn't understand that."

Noreen swished the vodka in her squat glass by making a circular motion with her hand. I only knew it was vodka because I had seen her pouring it before. We began to walk together. Away from the house.

"You sound happy that Logan left."

"No, I'm not," I said. "He seemed like a good worker."

"He was. And he was strong," said Noreen. "The people who would visit here liked to see him tending the horses on the field. He was like something out of a magazine. A Ralph Lauren ad or something. But he was a good worker besides all that. Anyway, I heard what he did to you."

I didn't say anything. I wasn't mad about it anymore, surprising even myself.

"He punched you right here," and Noreen raised a hand to rub my cheek.

The palm of her hand felt soft on my cheek. Her hands were soft, feminine, and cold like Miss Bouverie's. They were not a working person's hands. She left her hand against my face for what seemed like a prolonged period. I pulled her hand down and we began walking again. We were nearing the stables where I had shot the mare. The wind had picked up and it slammed a shutter against the wooden walls of the building. "I let Logan fuck me over there," Noreen said. "Not in the stable but in the shed next store where we keep the instruments. That's where the farrier goes when he stops by."

We heard tapping behind us, and we both turned around. It was Mino pacing on the concrete walkway behind the house. He watched us and his boots tapped loudly. He was holding down his cowboy hat on his head with one hand as men do. He was in good physical shape, as Logan had been. He looked to be about 190 pounds. I figured that because he looked like he weighed about the same as me. I was about 190. We heard one of the agriculturists come out of the house soon afterward and Mino got to talking to him. Noreen told me that she had to host the agriculturalists in her community every so often because she was the richest person in Thibault County. "You have to sow the seed," she told me, whatever that meant. Those were her words. Mino disappeared after that, but we heard him later: yipping at a mare that had broken free.

I went into the shed with Noreen. It was clear that she had intended me to go in with her. That's why she mentioned that she'd been with Logan in there. The shed wasn't locked. It had an unpainted, warped door, so I was able to see in through the cracks. I saw flecks of sharp light of various colors like the marbles that kids play with. Noreen had a hard time with the door even though it was unlocked. It was stuck and she really had to push hard to swing it open. "Let me help," I offered. "No, I got it," she said. She turned back to smile at me. She still had her hair dyed that warm auburn, but I saw her dark brown roots coming in. They were coming in quick. The door swung open with a bang. Noreen walked hesitantly over to a corner, and I heard the rattle of the kerosene lamp when she picked it up. She didn't need a match to summon the light. The lamp was cut on by a switch on the side. She cut the kerosene lamp on and told me to shut the door. "I'm so glad Odette sent you," she said. It rattled my cage to have Noreen speak my employer's name here.

As I walked deeper into the shed with Noreen, I saw that the space was filled with the carcasses of stuffed birds. They were well-preserved. The birds were hanging from the two longer walls of the shed. They were all in flight, as if they were flying towards you. They were in all manner of garish colors. Bird feathers were colored by nature to camouflage them but also to attract mates. Somehow this room of stuffed birds in flight was the most frightening thing that I had ever seen. I found it hard to believe that Logan had made love to Noreen in here. But I believed it all the same. Noreen was looking very attractive in her cinch-waisted dress and there had been all those men ogling her before when she had placed herself in the center of their conversation circle. "Ha, ha, ha!" she'd laughed when one man had said something stupid. There was a long concrete table in the center of the shed, right below an overhanging falcon with golden-colored eyes. Noreen led me to the table. She raised the back of her long white dress and she placed her bare buttocks against the cold concrete. She took my hands and placed them on her hips. I saw that somewhat below a wall of birds, the farrier had left some of his instruments.

"No, not here," I told her.

"Why not?"

"I know you think I'm dumb."

"What does that have to do with anything?" Noreen asked, and then she laughed.

"I don't want to do it in here."

We returned to the house. Most of the men were leaving, but there were still a few hanging around smoking cigars. Their laughter rang throughout the house between puffs on their cigars. It was the hearty laughter of people who are guests at a rich person's house. Like they're putting on a show. I occasionally heard Mino's high-heeled boots tapping as he walked from one part of the house to another, talking with another man. There was something super-masculine about the sound of his boots. I understood why Noreen had hired him. Although I didn't want to sleep with her, the sound of Mino's boots and the thoughts of why she'd hired him irritated me. As I walked up the stairs to the second floor with Noreen, I saw a framed poster that I hadn't noticed before. It's from an opera called Swan Lake. The opera's about a woman who is able to transform herself.

We didn't do it right away when we got to Noreen's room. Making it like some people used to say in the old days. "Let's go upstairs and make it." She said she wanted to watch a movie. That may have seemed like a nice, polite thing to do to some people, but I knew she only wanted to create the mood. Like I was the easy high school girl and she was the boy. The television was set in a TV stand that was disguised to look like a typical bureau you would have in your bedroom. She opened the twin bureau doors and there was the huge TV. She put in the film she wanted to watch, and I sat beside her on the bed as the credits began to roll. It was the largest bed I had ever seen. It seemed like it was large enough for three people. I groaned when she reached into the bedside table and produced a large candle.

"Not those goddamn candles again," I said.

She said something ridiculous like, "You know you love it," but I can't remember because I could barely hear her. I told her I wasn't interested and stood up from the bed. She laughed, even tossing her head back to do so. But she became angry when she realized I wasn't playing around.

"Get back here," she said. "You're a fuck. That's it. A fuck."

I reached the bedroom doorway. I looked both ways because I didn't know the fastest route out of the house. There had to be a route that didn't involve running into Noreen's guests. There was the main staircase that led down to the front door and the backstair that led to the kitchen.

"No, no, no, come on," Noreen called. "I didn't mean that. I want you here with me. I don't care about those godforsaken candles. Come on, right here," and she patted the spot on the bed beside her.

I returned to the bedroom, sitting down beside Noreen on the bed. Noreen laughed and made small talk. At one point, she took out the Derringer she carried with her and placed it on the table. I asked her: "You planning on shooting me if I don't sleep with you?" She told me she wasn't. It was funny to think of her carrying her Derringer as she chatted happily with all those cattlemen. One wrong word and bang. Sometimes when she asked me a question and I answered, she would draw back dramatically as if surprised by my answer. It reminded me of that time that I had gone to a rodeo, but they already had too many men for the bronc-riding competition so they asked me to do a scene with another guy they'd cut from the competition. The scene was this: I lasso a beautiful woman walking across the bull ring, and as I follow the rope to her, she pulls away dramatically.

"Let's just lay in the bed for a while," Noreen said.

I began to take off my boots. These were my nice vaqueros, and they killed my feet as I'd been wearing them all day. I thought Noreen would help, but she didn't. Boots off, I laid in the bed beside her. I resigned myself to the idea of screwing her. The wind blew a tree just outside Noreen's window, and we heard the angry rustle of the leaves as they fell to the lawn. Beside the bed was the closet. I turned on my side to look as the closet door was open. I saw a maid's black uniform hanging on a spongy-foam hanger. "That's the housekeeper's," Noreen said. "You've never met her before. Rita. She comes twice a week. I had to get that thing specially cleaned and I forgot to put it back in her room." She maneuvered closer to me in the bed. "Take your shirt off," she said. I began to unbutton my shirt, the nice shirt that Miss Bouverie had wanted me to wear, and I tensed my abdominal muscles self-consciously so the deep grooves were visible. I tensed my abdominal muscles for a woman who saw me as no different than the contents of the room. The bedside table. The lamp. The chair. When my shirt was off, I folded it neatly and looked for a place to set it down. But Noreen took the shirt from me quickly and threw it roughly to the ground. I felt the heat of Noreen's body as she moved even closer, and I smelt the perfume in the conditioner she used to wash her hair. The bed didn't creak as Noreen moved closer since her body was so slim.

"Yes," Noreen said.

I felt her cold-as-ice hands against my muscles.

"Yes," she said again.

Noreen didn't notice when something moved in the bed beside her. She was so close to me in the large bed that there was room enough for a third person on the other side of her. A mirror hung in the room beside the window. In the mirror, I saw what had happened. In the mirror, I saw that a void had appeared in the bed, as if the bedcover and bedsheets and mattress had all been sucked in. Then the body of the bed began to reappear, but this time there was a woman wearing a long white dress lying atop it. The dress came all the way down to the woman's ankles. The woman's feet were small and dainty. Noreen didn't see the woman, and she laughed in her enjoyment of me. Like the football captain laughs when he's about to screw the easiest girl in school. She playfully unbuttoned the top button of my jeans and then buttoned it again. "You're just an easy lay," she said, "Like Logan." The woman wearing the dress sat up. She was beside Noreen, but Noreen didn't see her. She had her back to her. I knew it was Miss Bouverie. Miss Bouverie threw her legs over the side of the bed and stood up. She didn't reach for the Derringer. She picked up the lamp. She yanked hard enough to rip the cord from the socket. That's when Noreen became aware of her. She gasped, but it was too late. Miss Bouverie raised the lamp high in the air and bludgeoned Noreen in the face with it. She bludgeoned her again and again.

8

I ran into Logan on the way home. His truck pulled up behind me at a gas station. He got out and told me that Jean was staying at a hotel outside of town. He wore a cattleman's leather jacket, and he didn't seem to hold a grudge. When I reached Jean's room in the hotel, I knocked on the door even though it was ajar. "Come in," she said. When I found her, she was crying by the TV. She told me that she'd been sick, and she'd had to go to the hospital. She hadn't run away. All the same, she didn't seem inclined to return to the ranch. The ER doctor paged the hematologist, and the latter told Jean that she'd had some internal bleeding some time ago, but it was mostly resolved. She'd have to return to see him in a follow-up appointment. Jean hadn't been to a hematologist in a long while as she didn't have insurance. She couldn't afford the follow-up appointment the hematologist wanted. It seemed strange to me that we had a hematologist in town. I told Jean that I had money from Hannah's estate, and I could pay for her appointment. With the tests it was almost $1000. She stood up and hugged me. Falling into my arms more or less. We heard horse hooves clopping outside. It sounded like a team of horses. As the hotel was so old-fashioned, it gave everything a bygone quality. Jean wept in my arms. Her face settled into the muscular cleft in my chest. I think that's the most impressive part of my body. By the time we went to the window, the horses had already gone.

57

9

"It was my husband's idea to move out of the city and purchase a ranch. We both worked in advertising and were ready for a change, so we decided to move back to the rural area where he was brought up. He was the youngest of three sons raised on a cattle ranch. His father's ranch was the largest in the county before it was sold. I had been brought up around the ranching life too: horse-riding and roping. I had learned to rope as I girl, which seems like many years ago. Once my husband bought the ranch, he decided he'd like to go back to the old way of life around here with cowboys, cattle and horses. Some ranches have shifted more towards pickups and ATVs, but he didn't want that. He knew how to break horses as his father had taken him down to learn the art on his uncle's ranch in Mexico. It was all very traditional. He was taught to break the potrillos, the untamed horses, and then transport the remudas into Texas where they'd be working horses. A remuda is just the name for a herd of tamed horses from Mexico. Since my husband was concerning himself with the cattle, he left me to tend to the care of the horses. Though I was familiar with horses, I was certainly out of my depth. I don't know what I would have done if it weren't for Bygone Ranching Life magazine. You ran an article about keeping working horses on large-scale ranch operations, and that was exactly what I needed. We raise a seed stock breeding herd, and we have cowboys to keep the herd in a traditional way. Your article covered everything

from how many ranch hands a seed stock ranch would require to recommendations on where to purchase the horses. You even meandered into whether to breed working horses or to buy them. I couldn't have asked for a better tutorial."
- Heather M., Bronc Run Ranch, Thibault County, Texas

Dickson is a small community lying in a sparsely-populated county of abandoned ranches and farmland. Dickson isn't the only community in the American Southwest to become a ghost town as a result of the young fleeing for better opportunities elsewhere, but it is remarkable for the seeming pall of poverty that overlays a region notable for its natural resources. Silver and iron ore were mined here after the Civil War, and there are known petroleum deposits that were tapped well into the 1970s. This was the heyday of Dickson, when oil barons and cattle kings called the town and its surrounds home. The large houses in the town bear testament to this time, even if the old families no longer reside here. These stately homes have been converted mostly into apartments, condominiums and rooming houses. The records at the local historical society attest to the abandonment of the area by the old gentry of the community. This and other demographic factors have left Dickson as practically a ghost town, with a population half of what it was in 1971.

The demographic collapse in Dickson is significant enough that local authorities have contemplated shutting down the local high school. Enrollment numbers at all of the local schools have dwindled to a trickle, and this is most telling at the high school, where there are nearly as many teachers and staff as there are students. The school, with its proud, brick-faced facade overlooking a manicured lawn of rolling grass, was impressive when first opened in the 1960s. We are told that the lawns around the school are planted with a species of grass developed locally by the ranching elite. Though the county coffers were supposed to have paid for the high school, local legend attests to the ranchers who opened their pockets to contribute most of the funds for the school building. While visiting the school, staff from Bygone Ranch Life were told that although the ranches for which the community was known have mostly gone, there was still one remaining. This was the Dancing Horse Ranch, which has been owned by the Bouverie family since World War I. The last member of the family, Miss Odette Bouverie, agreed to meet with us at her ranch, about ten miles outside of the center of Dickson. Miss Bouverie, a winsome woman of about thirty-five, very politely obliged to meet us considering her fragile state of health. Miss Bouverie suffers from arthrogryposis as a result of Schmallenberg infection, which she contracted from local cattle as a child.

At one time, Dancing Horse Ranch was one of several expansive estates lying on the outskirts of Dickson. These ranches provided seasonal employment to members of the Dickson community and food for their tables. At the center of Dancing Horse Ranch lies the big house, or simply the house, which once was presided over by a suitably-attired steward. The last steward of the house was Palmer Merriman, who left approximately ten years ago when the present owner of the ranch inherited the place from her father. The ranch had been compelled to downsize as a result of economic hardship and the need to economize. Dancing Horse Ranch had formerly hosted an agricultural stewardship class with the local 4-H as well as a large, well-attended agricultural fair, where local agriculturalists displayed their wares. The ranch was forced to end these long-established practices. The herd of steers and heifers was reduced to 80% of its former number, then 60%, and it has continued to dwindle. But the ranch acreage remains intact at about 10,000 acres. And the owner of the ranch, Miss Bouverie, has rejected attempts to stimulate the local Dickson municipality (population, 1115) by selling some of the land to build a shopping center. We learned most of this from Babette Spencer, daughter of a long-time resident of Dickson, who now works for Miss Bouverie as a cook. When one of our cameramen jokingly asked Babette if she was the daughter of that Flatfoot Spencer who was a notorious local bank robber, the lady demurely declined to answer.

At Dancing Horse Ranch, I sat with Miss Bouverie in a sitting room in her commodious, but outwardly modest house. Babette poured us refreshing cups of sweet tea as we gazed below at the broad, happy vista sprawled out before us. The tea is not nearly as sweet as the honeyed surrounds, humorless and in decline though they may be. The sky here is blue-gray and vague, and it seemed as if it looked down solely on this spot. In the far distance were the hands tending the cattle astride their working horses. Above the fireplace hung a portrait of Miss Bouverie's great-grandfather. He was the man who built the present ranch house. He was known to keep herds of over 700 head and to himself go out roping steers with his workers, sleeping outside under the unforgiving night sky with the rough working men. Miss Bouverie spoke openly about the great-grandfather whom she had known as a girl and whom she says taught her the importance of stewardship.

"The welfare of all things on the ranch is the responsibility of the ranch owner," Miss Bouverie said. "And that includes the cattle, the horses and all the people that live and work here. Naturally, the numbers of all these have dropped since my great-granddaddy's time, but the ranch lives on."

"Do you mind if I inquire more on that subject, Miss Bouverie?" I asked the lady.

"You may call me Odette."

"Yes, thank you. Odette, what do you see as the biggest challenge for ranching life in present day America? And is it possible to preserve this way of life for future generations?"

"The biggest challenge for our ranching life is the disconnect between modern day man and the land. People live in cities. People drive to the supermarket or to the fast-food restaurant, and they obtain their meat without the labor of their own hands. But in this community, we know that these things come from the hardworking men and women on ranches like these. People who rope cattle and ride horses. Out there you can see some of the horses we have on this property. These beautiful animals are not part of the daily lives of most people. So the biggest challenge is keeping our way of life visible when many people simply don't know that we exist. Of course, there are also the challenges of increasing population, competition from foreign countries, and the rising costs of labor due to inflation. All of these place additional pressures on me as a ranch owner."

"You seem to have a suitably pragmatic understanding of the challenges."

"I would say that that I do," said Odette.

"Any last words for us, Odette?"

"You know, it isn't easy being a ranch owner, and it's especially difficult when you're dealing with an illness like Schmallenberg. There are those that tell me that it's time to sell off, to move someplace else and leave the hard business to more able men. But how can I when I am the last of my family? And you know what? My great-granddaddy bought this ranch after making a fortune in the oil business. He was a hardworking man who came from nothing and turned that nothing into something. The story goes that he won 2000 acres of land in a poker game, if you can believe that. He was hard-up for money, so on a whim he decided to tap the land for oil. I reckon you can figure out the rest. He was a self-made man at a time when most of the men were that way. I had talks with him when I was young and he used to tell me: 'Odette, if a cow don't want to give you milk, you better twist those teats 'til she spits it out.' And that's precisely what I plan to do. At the moment, I'm unable to get my hands dirty with all the work on the ranch because of my illness, but I know that I'll get well. I shall someday. And once I'm well, I'll take up active management of the ranch again. I'll be able to get my hands dirty with all the heavy stuff. And I can go back to killing people and turning them against one another. I'll have my strength back. And then maybe I'll go on a nice, long trip."

10

I married Jean in Piedras Negras, where an old couple said we looked like brother and sister. We had the same doleful look. That must have been what they saw. We married in the Church of Our Lady of Guadalupe, where we convinced a few locals to serve as witnesses. We had gotten our papers before we'd come to Mexico, and Jean used what little Spanish she had to ensure that our marriage would be legal in the States. She'd worn a long white dress with a lace collar and a lace hem. Her face had been covered with a veil, and as I raised it I smiled at the thought that I had lassoed her at last.

We returned to the hotel from the church. The windows in the hotel room were protected by screens to keep the mosquitoes out, but the screens had holes in them. That night, Jean put her wedding dress back on and decided to walk the town. I followed her. There wasn't anything to see but many old churches. We went to a different church than the one we'd married in, and there we found a priest talking to himself and swinging a censer. He was limping the dark, lonely aisles. Jean and I sat in the front pew of the church with our heads bowed. The next day, we prepared to return to Texas. At the gas station, Jean told me she wanted to write a book about her family, but she couldn't decide what to write about. It was all so depressing, and she wanted to be happy. From now on, she would be happy. A man at the gas station, an American, told us there was a town not far from us where we might visit an old, deconsecrated monastery. The monastery had been surrounded by a village at one point in time, but some vigilante had shot the whole village up and now there was solely the monastery. It wasn't easy to reach, so we had to find a man named Nacho and ask him to lead us.

We found Nacho in town, standing outside one of the restaurants. He was easygoing and had nothing to do. With what little English he had, he told me used to be a cowboy in Coahuila. He used to break the potrillos before the horse dealers took them into Texas to sell. He was happy to show us the way to the monastery. His English wasn't the greatest, but it was passable. He politely pretended not to notice how beautiful Jean was. At one point, he told us we had to leave our car in the hills and go the rest of the way on donkeys. So we did. When we reached the monastery, we realized that the story the man had told us about the vigilante was true. The monastery was surrounded by alleys of houses, but all the windows in the houses had been torched out and the walls had bullet holes in them.

We returned to Texas, where our Peugeot coupe got a flat tire. The pickup I'd driven to Mexico had broken down, and I had been forced to buy an old Peugeot down there. I abandoned the pickup. But the coupe was cheaper than I thought it'd be. The Mexican men at the repair shop smiled and made conversation with me. I just left the truck with them. It wasn't difficult getting back into Texas. The landscape was the same as it had been in Northern Mexico, though we felt a new sense of freedom. We passed a town where I had long ago worked in a factory. This was one of the towns we had to pass through on the way to Hannah's house. It was my house now. The house sat in a sparsely-populated community, and was reached by an endlessly long dirt road. The road dived into a forest, but after about a mile all the trees disappeared. The land was flat and thirsty, and in the distance were the hills.

In the distance were the hopes that had died because people no longer believed in them. We came to a ranch-style house dwarfed by the hills in the distance. We rang the doorbell. A woman came to the door. Her long dark hair was in a pony-tail, and she wore a mantilla over her shoulders. I said hello to the woman and told her that we were trying to reach Hannah Anderton's house, that is, the house that Hannah Anderton had lived in before she die, but we'd managed to get lost. The woman knew it was down one of these dirt roads. Gabrielle. That was her name. She said that she'd be happy to show us the way, but first we ought to come in and have coffee. Gabrielle had dark eyes and the sexy air of a French actress.

Gabrielle led us into the kitchen, where a low table was surrounded by three chairs. A man's cowboy hat hung from a rung on the wall. Jean and I sat silently and waited for the woman to prepare the coffee using a French press machine. When she was done, she poured the coffee into three heavy ceramic cups. The coffee was rich and thick like hot chocolate. On the surface of the table was a lady's magazine from one or two years ago. Before she sat down to join us, Gabrielle took her Colt Python out of her pocket and rest it atop the surface of the table. The Colt rattled when she bumped into the table in the action of sitting down. She asked us what we did to support ourselves.

Jean said: "I just left my job. I think I'll focus on home things now. Kip says the house hasn't been cleaned, so I think I might have to work on it a bit."

"And what about you?" Gabrielle asked, glancing quickly at me.

"I'm a ranch manager. Well, I used to be," I told her. "I used to be a bronc rider."

"You look like you used to be a competitive bodybuilder."

"No, Ma'am, but I've done all sorts of things. At the moment, I'm waiting for some money to come in. When it does, I hope I can get my own ranch."

"So you want to be a rancher."

"Yes, Ma'am."

"And for now you're finding ways to keep busy."

"Right. I'm thinking about doing some investing."

"What kind of investing?"

"Just traditional stocks."

"You must've saved up quite a bit from bronc riding."

"No, actually. Not a dime. I have a little from an inheritance."

Jean explained to Gabrielle that I had been married to Hannah.

Gabrielle led us through the environs after that. As soon as we turned onto the dirt road that led to Hannah's house, I recognized where we were. We passed a number of abandoned-looking houses and finally we came to Hannah's house. Gabrielle left after that, promising to visit us at some point in the coming weeks. She said as we were just married, she'd leave us time to settle in. She didn't mind walking back to her house as we had driven in my Peugeot.

After Gabrielle left, I realized that the door to Hannah's house was locked and I didn't have the key. I glanced around for another way in. I contemplated breaking in, but Jean said we'd better not. Someone might hear. "It's strange coming back to house that someone died in," she said. I told her that it wasn't like anyone had been murdered in the house. Hannah hadn't been murdered, at least not that anyone could prove. And the house had been basically cleaned by the executor of Hannah's estate. Peering through the window, we saw the old wallpaper and personal things on tabletops. There wasn't any reason to be afraid, I told Jean.

We went to the house closest to Hannah's property, a house which was more than fifty feet away. This wasn't the house where Max, Hannah's neighbor, lived but the house on the other side. The house we went to was nicer and older than Hannah's: a tall brick building with exposed woodwork. It was out of place for the neighborhood, but the grass on the lawn was overgrown. I knocked on the door. "Hello," I said, but no one came to answer. There was a turned-on lamp in the front hall behind the door. I knocked a second time, and the door crept open with a loud creak.

"No, Kip, don't," said Jean, but she followed me in all the same.

She followed me past the entry hall and the kitchen to the master bedroom. The house was covered in wood-paneling so shiny that you could almost see your reflection in it. The door to the master bedroom was open and I walked into the room with Jean. The room had shag carpeting and a bed large enough for four people. Behind the bed was a door to the walk-in-closet. The closet wasn't locked. Jean followed me in and she was shy as I went through the belongings. The guns. The rawhide jackets. The fur coats. "Don't," she said, as I opened a drawer built into the wall. When I opened it, I found some pill bottles and beneath that was the expensive jewelry.

"Come over here," I told Jean.

She came hesitantly, like a girl that had been naughty, and she turned around because she knew what I was going to do. I took a fur coat down from the wall and I put it over Jean's spaghetti-strap blouse.

"We shouldn't be doing this," she said. "This is someone's stuff."

"Who cares?"

I walked with Jean over to the mirror in the master bed-room. I showed Jean how beautiful she was. She turned to face me. She let her fingers run down the grooves in my abdomen. She could touch them because one of the lower buttons in my flannel shirt had become unbuttoned. I was still shooting myself up with winstrol and equipoise. There was some question about the purity of the Mexican drugs, but I still looked pretty good. Jean informed me of her opinion that Gabrielle was interested in me. She said a woman always knows. She told me I shouldn't have told Gabrielle that I used to ride bulls. That's what had turned her on. I said: "Maybe I should have told her I used to work at a textile mill." Jean laughed. In the mirror, she surveyed the shape of her body: the narrow waist that curved down to slim, but womanly hips. I held Jean's hair up with my hand because she looked sexier like that. Hair held up by a man and wearing a fur coat. Like something expensive. Like the most expensive mare in the freight car. The fur coat hung just barely from Jean's shoulders. You could see the shape of her through her clothes. The high breasts with their large areolas. Jean became transfixed by her own image. She didn't see the silhouette of Odette drawing nearer to her in the mirror. By the time she realized, Odette was already upon her.

11

The next day I drove into the nearest town, which was about a half hour away. I was able to get the key to Hannah's house from a safety deposit box in my name. Then I went into the local convenience store to see if I could buy a newspaper, but the clerk told me that the local paper had closed business more than a year before. He laughed.

<h1 style="text-align:center">12</h1>

I awoke one morning to find Jean staring out the bedroom window. This was two days after we settled into Hannah's house. The window looked out on the 40-some-odd acres of land behind the house. The land was silent. Sometimes we heard people driving on the dirt road. We could hear them talking with the windows down, but they never had anything important to say. There were trees in the neighborhood but scarcely any on Hannah's land. The neighborhood was free from any feature aside from the abandoned things one came across: the unused tires piled up by the roadside and the turned-over Scania flat bed. I sat up on one arm and watched Jean as she gazed out the window. Noticing me, she said she was just settling into the place. This was her way of settling in. We'd have to find a grocery store or a butcher since there wasn't anything in the house. She camouflaged how she felt with small talk. I asked her if she'd noticed that shed in the back, about halfway to the property line. That was where Hannah used to tie up her horses. And even further back from that was a rusty old swing. The horses had been sold after Hannah died.

Jean got to work in the kitchen after returning from the butcher's. Though she was sick, and I thought of her always as being a sick, she was at her best when she was doing things. She cleaned the dishes that Hannah had left in the house, and she left the meat on a cutting board in the kitchen to defrost it. All afternoon I heard the sound of the water running from the faucet. I went up to the upstairs bathroom to inject my-self. I had bought several weeks' worth of veterinary steroids in Mexico. They were better than nothing. These compounds would be more potent than what I was used to taking if any-thing. I didn't know where Rob was. I'd tried calling him. I glanced at myself in the bathroom mirror. The mirror was scratched and there were blackened spots where the glass had completely eroded. But I still saw my barn-door-wide shoul-ders. The thick vein snaking from my right clavicle down my arm. I thought I looked pretty good.

Jean came up to find me once dinner was on. It was cooking on the stove. She put her arms around me and I pulled pants up. She ran her hands over my chest. I still had a tan from Mexico.

"Stop," I told her. "My nipples are real sensitive right now."

"It's from the stuff you're taking," she remarked.

"I need to get this drug called Clomid," I told her, but I didn't explain what it was.

We left the bathroom. I told her the layout upstairs was strange because Hannah had rented the upstairs as a second apartment. There had been a girl who lived up here named Martha who moved out after Hannah died. That's why there was a second kitchen up here. But the kitchen was only as large as a closet, which is what it had been before. There was a room that Jean had tried to get into, but it wouldn't budge. "It's not locked. You just have to push the door," I told Jean. I ran into it with my shoulder and it busted open with a loud bang.

"Careful, you'll get splinters," Jean said.

I stood aside to let Jean enter. I already knew what was in there.

"Oh Lord," Jean said.

Hung on a wall inside the room were half a dozen deer heads. These had been big bucks with majestic, fierce antlers. The bucks' eyes were glassy like you see in preserved animals.

The walls of the room didn't have any wallpaper. Most of the house was papered in this yellow print that Hannah liked. Jean stood partially in the room and glanced inside. Her eyes darted from one corner to another. I told Jean I didn't know what Martha did for a living when she asked me. But what I did know was that her boyfriend was a hunter. This was the boyfriend she was always fighting with on the phone. It had been him who had hunted the deer and mounted them on the wall. There was a desk and chair opposite the wall of buck heads, so I figured Martha had used this room as an office. I told Jean so. "It's terrible," Jean said. I asked her what was so terrible about it. "It's just terrible," she said. I told her it wasn't, and I pushed her in the room. I closed the door tightly, knowing Jean wouldn't be able to open it from inside.

"Kip, no," said Jean. "Let me out. This isn't funny."

"Yes, it is," I told her. "There's nothing to be scared of."

"But I don't like it."

"They're dead, Jean. What, you think those bucks are gonna come back to life and trample you to death?"

"Kip, stop," said Jean softly.

Then she was quite for a minute or two. I didn't hear a peep out of her. Eventually I heard the tap of her feet on the plank floor. She was pacing the room. But then those taps stopped too and it was silent again. I imagined Jean was standing with her back to the deer. I forced the door open after about two minutes. Jean wouldn't look at me at first. She didn't move, but soon she turned and began walking towards me.

"I'm mad at you," she said.

She beat a fist playfully on my chest.

"I know, Jean. I'm sorry," I told her.

"I don't why I married you," Jean said. But then she looked up at me to show that she was kidding.

When we met Jackson later, he told me that he and Jean had begun dating when she transferred into his high school. She had to transfer because she'd moved in with another foster family. One of the assistant coaches on the football team had told Jackson that Jean was a nice girl who was sure to be harried by the boys in the school because she was new and pretty. The coach had gotten that idea from someone else who'd told him to look out for Jean. In all places, people talk and do things like that. The right thing for Jackson to do, said the coach, was to ask Jean to go steady. That would force the boys to wander off to some other girl. Jackson and Jean wouldn't do anything romantic. They would just be known to all to be going steady. Jean would be accepted by the others. The boys would leave her alone.

Jean said little at dinner. She played with the paperweight we'd found on the kitchen table. It was the kind you shake and it makes a blizzard. It was a gift that Hannah had bought to remind herself that she'd go away one day, but she never did. She never left the dirt roads in the town. The roads didn't seem to lead anywhere.

"I wonder if Odette will write," Jean said after we'd finished most of dinner.

"Is that what we're calling her now?"

"That's her name, isn't it?"

"We don't need to talk about her," I offered.

"No, we don't, but maybe we should," said Jean. "I'm certain I saw her car parked out back when I woke up in the middle of the night. I felt the headlights on my face through the window and I saw her Ford out on the back lawn. That same Ford as before. You know how it is when you feel the heat of a car's lights on your face. The high beams."

"Jean, don't."

"It was her. She's following us. And she didn't even bother to write. No severance pay, no nothing. She just let us go."

"Well, it's no surprise she doesn't write when one of us thinks she's a monster."

"She doesn't know what I think," said Jean. But then Jean smiled at me. She had a way of looking sweetly at you when she smiled. It was the thing I missed the most after we destroyed her.

"No, she doesn't know what I think," Jean went on. "How could she? And besides, I don't think that she's a monster. Not a literal one. I don't know what I think. I just know it was her I saw."

Jean looked out the narrow kitchen window. I thought Jean was watching the road for signs of horses. There were no horses here and we felt the absence of them. There was no indication of them at all. The road meandered down to the woods.

Jean received a letter from Jackson a week after we'd settled into the house. "Lookie here at what I got," she said. She was walking into the living room. I was sitting in a corner of the room with my unshod feet atop the turned-off woodburning stove. I wore the kind of thick wool socks where the neck of the sock is a different color from the foot.

"What is it?"

Jean waved Jackson's letter at me, but she didn't hand it to me to read. She was being playful like a kitten. That's an old-fashioned thing to say, but she was. She gave me the gist of it. An old friend of hers called Jackson had heard that we'd recently moved into town and that we'd just married. He invited us to visit him at his place. He lived back in the woods outside of town. You could hardly call it a town at all. Frame houses all run up together broken up by the occasional farm. Dirt roads. Dairy cattle grazing in front of farmhouses. In the farmhouses, handsome young boys and girls had their hopes dashed when they got pregnant young and became alcoholics.

Handsome young boys borrowed their father's shotguns and blew their brains out. Or they borrowed their father's horses and rode with their girlfriends somewhere far. When I met

Jackson later and saw how he looked like a man from a magazine, I wondered how he'd escaped. He looked like the boys who tried to escape but didn't. Only he hadn't really escaped. Jackson was taller than average, and his roundish face was covered in a week-old beard. It's the kind of beard a man grows when he wants to appear masculine to women. The hairs of his chin couldn't fully hide the cleft. His eyes were dark blue. His hair was a little too sharp (he had just gotten it cut), but the week-old beard kept him from looking too proper. Jackson always wore dark-colored flannel shirts. When he smiled, his fleshy lips parted to reveal perfect teeth. His teeth weren't chipped from being thrown by a bronc like mine were. Roping, branding, castrating. We reached Jackson's property by taking a back road through the woods. At one point, I had to step out of the Peugeot and push open a rusted metal gate that blocked the way. The car I'd bought was a Peugeot 205, which is a very small car. A magazine named this contraption Car of the Decade in 1990. After passing through the gate, you drove down a baleful road and soon caught sight of the house. The house was approached by an alley of old oak trees. There was no other place in the area with twisted trees like these.

Jackson was standing on the porch when we rounded the bend. He came down the steps just as we were pulling the car in front of an old shed. Polite like Noreen had been before. There were never any garages at old houses like these. Jackson hugged Jean warmly when he reached us. Me he acknowledged with a handshake. I squeezed his hand hard and rough, but that was just my way. His palms were calloused as a man's should be. A working man's hands. The halls in the house all sang. That is to say, they creaked. We took a hall to get to the parlor. The parlor was the largest, fanciest room in the house. It had green wallpaper with flecks of gold. We passed a room full of expensive china to get there. "I didn't buy any of this stuff," Jackson said. Jackson had bought this house before moving back to the area. He'd bought it sight unseen. All the contents inside had come with the house as the owners had died long ago.

"Did you hear what happened to Keri?" Jackson asked Jean. We were all seated at table by then.

"Yes, I heard," said Jean in a sing-songy way. "She married that guy from the gas station. Didn't his father used to own that store down the road from our school? That general store? For the life of me, I can't remember his name."

"John LaFleur."

"That's right. LaFleur. He must be almost 10 years older than us," Jean said.

"He's not that much older. I think he's about five years. They have a kid now."

Jackson spoke between bites from his steak. He'd used his steak knife to cut big, manly pieces. It felt like he was cutting pieces of Jean's body and bringing them up to his lips. That's what he seemed to be doing as I sat there watching him. Like she belonged to him. I wondered how long the steroids I bought from Mexico would last.

"He must be six years old by now," said Jean. She'd hardly touched her food. She didn't eat the steak at all. She'd had some of the green beans and mash at the beginning of the meal.

"I think the kid's seven," said our host. Jackson didn't slather the steak in steak sauce as some men do. He poured the steak sauce down on a corner of his plate and dabbed it politely with his fork. "They married about eight years ago. It was right out of high school practically. I think Keri was a sophomore at A&M."

"That's right," said Jean. "It was sophomore year."

"It's a boy. He's a cute kid. Caleb, I think. He's gotta be seven years old by now," Jackson said. Then he turned to me. "I'm sorry, Kip. I'm not one to gossip, but it's been so long since I've seen Jean."

"No need to apologize. I understand."

"Kip doesn't mind," said Jean. "He understands how old friends need to catch up."

"I sure do."

"I can't believe you bought this place," said Jean.

"So you know the story," Jackson said, looking down at his plate.

"No, I don't," said Jean. "What story?"

"The old Hansen place," I said, cutting in.

"Kip knows the story," said Jackson. "Evidently."

"What's the old Hansen place?" Jean asked. "I mean, the significance?"

"The old Hansen place," I repeated. "It was an old story when I used to live around here. That's how old it is. Gruesome."

"It ain't that bad," and Jackson laughed.

"It is, Jack," I said. "People died here."

"Oh Lord," said Jean.

"Do people call you Jack?" I asked, but I already knew the answer.

"Nobody calls me Jack. Well, you can if you want, Kip, since we're friends now, but no one else calls me that."

"Nobody except for Mr. Lefinger," said Jean. She sipped her pink lemonade mischievously. Jackson had recollected that pink lemonade was Jean's favorite drink, and he had gone to purchase some before we came over. He told us that as we were sitting down to dinner.

"Who's Mr. Lefinger?" I asked, looking at Jean and Jackson in turn. They both laughed.

"His name was actually Mr. Lefevre but everyone called him Mr. Lefinger," Jackson explained.

He went on to tell his story. All the sound went out of the room as I watched him and Jean recollecting old times. They were speaking, that is, their lips were moving, but all I heard was the deafening hiss of the insects outside.

"So a student started a story that Mr. Lefevre wanted to do certain things to these guys," said Jackson. I could suddenly hear him again. "Then everyone started calling him Mr. Lefinger. It wasn't very nice."

"Well, he wasn't exactly the nicest person, Jackson," said Jean.

"Hell, you ain't wrong about that," said our host. "Do you know he tried to get my scholarship to Galveston revoked? He told the football coach there that I had a bad character."

"Some people are like that," said Jean. "I think we've all had to deal with people like that in our lives. And there's hardly anyone less deserving of being called bad than you. You know that."

"Thanks, Jean," said Jackson.

It grew late and Jackson invited us to stay the night. Our place was less than thirty minutes away, but the road wasn't lit, and the polite thing to do was to invite us to stay the night. So that's what Jackson did. We could hardly refuse. And he said the next morning he'd take us to a diner he knew nearby. The place was famous for their root beer. Jackson said root beer made him break out, but he'd take us anyway. It was worth the acne to have good root beer once in a while. And then there was the diner's famous baby back ribs. Then Jackson led us up to the room that Jean and I would share together. His boots made a heavy thud as we went up the stairs. He didn't lead us halfheartedly. He had to carry a kerosene lamp since he said the hall light upstairs was so dim. He'd get it fixed in time. He'd fix it himself. Jean walked beside him as we traveled the hall, and the lamp set off the red accents in her hair. Her natural color was a dark auburn brown, but there were strands that were redder than the rest.

Jackson opened the door for us when we reached our room. He held it open for us to walk in. Jean walked in first and I followed her. She was dressed plainly today. I was too. She wore a white skirt that came down to below her knee, like she was going to visit someone's mother. On the wall in the corridor was a painting of a hunter lying dead in a dale with his rifle beside him. A fawn looked guiltily on.

"You two are still close," I said to Jean as she turned down the bed covers to make readiness for bed.

"Kip, stop," said Jean.

The bed looked as if it had been made by a professional. Jackson was nothing if not full of surprises. I imagined his large hands struggling to tuck the ends of the bedcover under the mattress.

"Nothing wrong with you just admitting it," I said.

"There's nothing to admit."

"Sometimes we can't help but have a feeling for people who were in our lives at the important stages," I said. "It's like we associate them with a time when we were young. Vulnerable."

Jean stopped what she was doing and turned to glance at me. She said: "That's an unusually perceptive thing to say."

"You mean an unusually perceptive thing to say coming from me."

"No, that isn't what I meant at all," said Jean.

"I know you think I'm dumb, Jean."

"I don't think that."

"I'm not."

The bedroom had a bathroom attached to it and I walked in. I had a look at myself in the mirror. I was looking haggard in the face. I hadn't had enough water to drink that day. Sometimes the steroids could leech the water out of your body. I wondered why Rob wasn't answering his phone. Then I ran the tap. As expected, the water pressure was low. "The water pressure's low," I said.

"Figures," Jean.

I splashed some water on my face. I cupped my hands and drank the water straight from the tap. I walked out of the bathroom to find Jean sitting on the edge of the bed. She was fidgety. She looked off. I asked her what had gotten into her, and she didn't tell me at first. Then she asked me about the house. I walked over to the window, which was blocked by heavy curtains. The curtains had those thick, ropelike bottoms like in the movies. Then I told her.

The house had belonged to a man who had made a fortune as an art dealer. Mr. Hansen. He sold reproductions of famous paintings all over the country. It was said that he'd passed off some of them as originals. That's how he'd grown so rich. But no one knew for certain, I told Jean. After making his money, the man had moved to Texas from Chicago. He'd always wanted to own a Texas ranch. He assembled small parcels of land in the middle of nowhere to create his homestead. It was a dream come true. He could breed horned cattle like he'd always wanted and fire his shotgun off in the air at night with no one to complain. Bang. He'd planned to live a simple, lonesome life, but then he met a beautiful woman. It isn't clear where she came from, this woman. Perhaps he met her on a business trip. He married her and brought her back to his Texas ranch. They settled into this big house, which was like several small houses put together in the middle of nowhere. It was Mrs. Hansen who furnished the house with all of its fine things: the fine china and silver and such. One day, Mr. Hansen didn't show for a court appearance, and when the sheriff came to visit some hours later, he found the bodies of Mr. and Mrs. Hansen, as well as that of a worker they'd hired to help on the place. Mrs. Hansen and the worker had both been shot in the face with a shotgun, while Mr. Hansen was found drowned in the above-ground pool near the stables. It was the pool that the horses drank from. The Hansens had also bred horses.

Jean didn't say anything. But a few minutes later she said: "Maybe we could go back home. We still have time."

"You're being ridiculous," I told her. "Jackson just brought us up here. He invited us to stay the night. It would be rude to leave."

The look Jean turned on me was wild. Her eyes were wild. But this wild look only lasted for a moment. All the same, things seemed to be passing as Miss Bouverie had predicted. Jean had a love interest, or what some might call a love interest, and there was something in the area to scare her. Jean was beautiful when she rose from the bed and came to me. My shirt was still off and I had a towel wrapped around my shoulders. When I turned around to look for some things I had left atop the dresser, Jean took a few steps more and wrapped her arms around my body. She rested her face against my back, where droplets of water and sweat had collected.

"No, don't," I said.

"I know, your nipples," Jean laughed.

I couldn't help but laugh too.

"Don't ever leave," she said. "Promise?"

"Who would I leave you for, darlin'?" I asked her.

"Odette."

"Why would I leave you for Odette?"

"I don't know," Jean said. "I don't know, but doesn't it feel like things are converging in an ominous way?"

"An ominous way, Jean?"

"Yes, something's off."

"Let's go to bed," I told her. I couldn't help but laugh again.

We got into bed after that. I slept facing the window, and Jean snuggled up behind me as she liked to do. The window faced the same bleak landscape that all the windows faced. A landscape where people traveled the dirt roads on foot or in pickups to gossip at other's people houses. There were people that wanted to run away, but there wasn't any escape. Boys shot themselves with their daddy's shotguns. Jean had an arm slung over me, and her head rest against my back. I felt her soft hair upon my shoulder. I felt her breath upon the muscles of my back. I was lying face-down. In the night, I awoke to see Jean standing beside the bed. From there, she walked towards the full-length mirror hanging along one wall. The mirror was heavy and had a golden frame. Jean was dressed in her nightie. She reached the mirror and stopped there, watching her feminine body with interest. She passed fingers through her hair in that slow, deliberate way that women do. She inspected her face. Her lips. Her cheekbones were high. This was a family trait. Jean had found some pictures to show me, and the other hemophiliacs of her family had these selfsame high cheekbones. Jean watched her face, her cheekbones, until her face began to change in the mirror. Her body changed too. She became Odette. Odette was taller and more seductively built than Jean. Odette's fawn-colored hair fell over her chest. The ends of her hair were the color of butter. Odette was smiling. She stepped out of the mirror: first one foot and then another. Jean no longer had any reflection as the woman that had been in the mirror had stepped out of it. Odette inspected a vase of dead flowers resting on a table. Then she set the vase down and walked over to my overnight bag. She rummaged through all the steroids and found the gun I carried. She found herself beside Jean and handed her the gun.

13

"Good morning, Chantal," I said to Jean when I got up.

We were back in Hannah's house. I threw my legs over the side of the bed and turned to glance at my wife. She sat by the window. There wasn't much to see out there. About a hundred feet off was the top of Max's house, set far back from the road, and then there was the overgrown field behind Hannah's house.

"That's not funny," Jean said, but she smiled.

I rose from the bed and walked to her. The chair Jean sat in was so small that she looked as big as Max sitting in it. But Jean wasn't like Max at all. If anything, the world was too wide for her. It was too mean.

"I was thinking we could leave the house today," I told Jean. "Go roam outside for a bit."

"In the Peugeot."

"No, not in the car," I said. "We'll go for a long stroll. We'll see where we end up. Like people used to do in the old days. The woods go back about a mile or two back from here."

"We can't get around these parts without a car," said Jean.

"We can. There are all kinds of back roads around here. There's even a road leading all the way to Dickson."

"Do you really want to?"

"Sure, darlin'. Why not?"

I injected myself with winstrol and equipoise before we left. Jean watched me. I wasn't of a mind to change my routine now that I was living here. The ranching life I'd had was gone, but I wasn't ready to give up on it just yet. I couldn't remember the last time I'd been out riding with Hunt. Roping, branding, castrating. When you got a new calf, you had to brand it so the other hands knew that it was yours. Yourn. I remembered when I was a boy my grandfather had a friend who would always say that. "Is that one of yourn?" he would say. If you didn't know which cow was yourn, you'd wind up coming home with fewer head than you left with. There might be a time where you grazed your herd on a field where other men grazed. Or you might take your cattle to a dealer for sale. You might get your herds mixed up.

Jean and I strolled for a time. I had my hat with me, which I used to swat away the flies when they came near. The flies were practically the size of men. It wasn't really true, but at times it felt that way. We passed the cluster of houses in the nearer section of town and came to an area of farms. We saw few people until we saw two men loading hay onto a truck. They spat out their chewing tobacco and said things to one another, but we couldn't hear them. We came to a road crossing after two miles and then a general store. There was the general store, a shut-up gas station and another shut-up building. I walked into the general store with Jean just as a man wearing chaps walked out. He stopped to look at Jean after we'd passed him. Then he lit up a cigarette. The man working the store wore chaps of smooth leather. He sold the sort of supplies that could be used on a ranch. He told us he sold feed too, which he stored in a small silo behind the store. I heard the water running in an irrigation canal behind the store. The man ran his hands under a faucet behind the counter because he'd dirtied them. I saw a rawhide jacket that had been made for a smallish man, but I thought it'd look good on Jean. I asked the man if I could take it down and have a look at it. I'd have to use a ladder to do so. He told me that I could.

"This was made for you," I told Jean.

She shook her head but tried it on when I handed it to her. I came down the ladder and stood beside Jean in the mirror. The red tones in her hair formed a stark contrast with the rawhide. Rawhide is just untanned leather. A long time ago, Ronald Reagan had Rawhide as a Secret Service codename. When I asked Jean if she knew why they'd called him that, she said she didn't know. "It's nice," Jean said, looking at herself in the mirror. "It's strange. I taught myself never to want anything. I learned to be happy with what I had. When I was a girl, I mean."

Wanting something you couldn't have was a sure way to sadden yourself. I had that experience of learning not to want things too, but I didn't tell Jean so. I had to keep some of myself separate from her. I hadn't yet accomplished what Odette wanted. I asked the man how much he wanted for the rawhide jacket and he told me I could get it for $120. I only had $100, and he was satisfied with that. We returned to the crossing where we came across a tied-up horse that we hadn't seen before. I told Jean this kind of horse was called a Missouri Fox Trotter. The horse was muscular and had white markings on its legs. I used to get white splotches on my legs when I was a boy that wouldn't go away. The mare warmed quickly to me when I offered her my hand. I told Jean we should ride her.

"But she isn't yours," Jean said.

She stood back as I unroped the mare. I reached a hand out to Jean when the mare was free and I was astride, and Jean took it. I helped Jean astride the horse. She had ridden horses before. We rode the horse along sloping ground away from the road. We turned an unfamiliar bend and rode the horse hard until we came to a stream. Jean's arms hugged me tightly. I felt the touch of her face against my back. When we came to the stream, I regretted that we hadn't brought any provisions with us. We might skewer meat and cook it as we'd done before with Kirk. Jean told me that she didn't want us to go back to that time. It was like a bruise that hadn't healed yet. I told her I didn't understand what she meant.

"You don't know what it means to be dependent on other people," Jean said. "To have nothing that's yours. I didn't want to be a maid. How could someone with hemophilia be a maid? I could fall. Anything might happen. But you take a job because you have to. Kip, my sister is 20 years older than me. I don't even think she likes me. But I was living with her until something else came up. And if that something else was to come up, then I had to do something. So be a maid it was."

"I don't follow."

"You take a job because you need the money. You stay at the job even if it isn't right. Even when you don't belong. I used to get so sick. And when you're sick, all the people you work for do is complain that your work isn't up to par. I don't think you know what it's like. You can't possibly know."

"Oh, I don't know what that's like," I said. "I've never been to work before. Not a day in my life."

"No, I didn't mean that," said Jean.

"It's all right, darlin'," I told her. "You had to pass through a hard period."

"Please don't bring her up."

"I won't." I chuckled. "You can't even say her name."

"Because it's like she's always with us. It's like her spirit has left her body in that bed and it's chasing after us."

"Chasing after us? Jean, come on."

We headed home when the sun began to set. The sky was rose-hued and bloody as I helped Jean astride the horse. We had left it roaming as we sat on the dirt to watch the sun. We knew it wouldn't wander far. It had grown dark quick and there were no streetlamps, but I knew the way. I knew the way in the fashion that a ranch hand always knows the way home. He just knows. He knows because there are people depending on him.

You might even say the cattle are depending on him. Roping, branding, castrating. We wouldn't go back to the crossing to return the mare that day. I'd have to take her back tomorrow. I told Jean they used to shoot horse thieves and string them up if they were caught. But I laughed as I told her so.

"You all right, Chantal?" I asked Jean as we joined the dirt road that led to Hannah's house.

Jean hugged me tightly as we rode the mare.

"Am I Chantal?" Jean asked herself.

14

I injected myself with equipoise and winstrol before I went to meet Jackson at his property. Jackson had called me up on the telephone. The land line had been disconnected after Hannah had died, but I'd gotten it reconnected. The first call I got was from Jackson. "Hey-yo!" he said like a character in a movie. And then he laughed in that cheerful way of his. It was hard to see him so happy knowing what was bound to happen. He was Jean's love interest. He ran out to meet me as the Peugeot barreled down the lane towards his house. "Hey, man," he said. "I guess you know why I called you out here." I didn't so I just shook my head. His handshake was warm and gentlemanly. He told me that he wanted to get into raising breed cattle. Seed stock. He figured I knew all about that so why not ask me. He stood wide-eyed as I told him about pens and heifers and steers and machines that the feed trammels down through. I told him he needed a good feed supplier because you can get raped if you have a bad one. Some of these guys will charge you twice the going rate for feed for the bottom-shelf stuff. And it's important to know how to castrate the bulls yourself. You just grab them by the balls and do it. Jackson was gazing intently at me and patting the front pocket of his flannel shirt, looking for something to write with. In his brown eyes, all I saw were hayrides and parties on abandoned farms. No one knows what happened to the farmers. There were roads running in front of and behind the farms, but the roads didn't lead anywhere.

When I got to Deirdre's office, there was a truck parked in the lot and a woman in a chinchilla coat sitting on the hood. There was something feral in the woman's beauty, as if she had adopted the spirit of the animals whose pelts she wore. The woman got in her husband's truck and drove off after the man returned. A couple of men who'd been sitting in their cars watching the woman got out and walked toward one another. They walked expectantly as men do when they're about to engage in idle talk. They discussed the woman animatedly and shook their heads as men do. The roof of the real estate office cast the men into shadow. The roof of Deirdre's real estate office was Dutch-gabled, and it stood apart from the dusty, haphazard single-floors of the rest of the town.

Walking in, I searched for Deirdre, but couldn't find her. Then a man sitting at a desk put down the receiver of the telephone he was speaking on and pointed towards an office to the left of where I stood. He said: "She's the owner so she's in the back office." I tipped my hat to the man and walked toward the office in question. I heard a woman's laughter and soon afterward the door swung open. I stood aside, but no one walked out. It seemed the woman had been on the telephone and she was alone. "Come in," she said. I dusted off the tops of my boots and walked in.

"Have a seat," Deirdre said.

I hadn't met her before, but she looked like her picture in the billboard I'd seen outside of town. She stood up to greet me.

"I know you said you'd drop in today, but somehow I wasn't expecting you," and Deirdre laughed, displaying her perfectly-shaped teeth.

"People don't show up when they're supposed to," I remarked.

"No, they don't," said Deirdre. "What brings you in today? I only got a vague idea from your call."

I cleared my throat and said: "I inherited some property from my late wife that I'd like to sell. It's a little involved because some of the estate is still in probate, but from what I can tell the commercial building isn't."

"No, it's not," said Deirdre. "I already looked. The only things in probate are the cash from your late brother-in-law's account, the money from his insurance policy, and his trailer. There's also the land the trailer sits on. The court could put a hold on the other property from your wife's estate if they determine that she owed money, but no one's stepped forward yet and I see no reason for the court to do that at present."

"I'm not sure I follow, Ma'am."

"The commercial property is free to sell for the time being, if that's what you're worried about."

"Ah, I see," I said.

At that point, Deirdre seemed to recall that she had wanted to water the plants in the office when I came in. There was a clear pitcher of water sitting atop her desk, and the walls of the office were lined with plants whose branches spilled out everywhere. If you wanted something in life you just had to take it. If you didn't like something because it was weak you destroyed it. The plants might one day break through the siding if they wanted to. Deirdre stood up and excused herself as she began to water the plants. She wore a white blouse with a lace collar over a cornflower-blue skirt. She wasn't wearing a bra. Her legs were long and correct like a filly's, and her head was perched on a long, muscular neck. "Go on," she said.

"Well, I was wondering too if your office helped with securing financing to invest in farm and ranching businesses," I told her. "I mean a kind of agricultural loan secured by the property."

"It's America. Of course there are loans available."

"I know," I said. "I'm not asking for myself. It's for a friend."

"You mean Jackson Riley."

"I didn't realize you knew him, Miss."

"It's a small town," said Deirdre. The water splashed out on the green, hungry bodies of the plants. The stems. "I knew about him before he even moved in. My understanding is that he doesn't need a loan because he's the beneficiary of a trust."

"No, that's not right. He made his money working out West."

"He might have made the money that he bought the house with, but he's still the beneficiary of a trust in his name. Maybe he doesn't want to use the money from the trust to invest in the ranch."

"Maybe."

"Anyway, I think we shouldn't have any problem listing your commercial property and finding a buyer. The building's at a busy intersection in town so it should sell quick. I'll just need to do some homework about a price, and I'll call you later once I've decided on something. That sound good?"

"That sounds good," I told her.

"And then I just need to convince these old knuckleheads around here to put out and buy the place," said Deirdre. "And then you can discuss it with your wife. How is she?"

"She's just fine. Thank you. A neighbor said they'd drop by today. They're probably wrapping up around now I bet."

"So, I'll let you go then," said Deirdre. She turned her back to me as she set down the water pitcher. She pulled out her chair gracefully like a woman who had been taught how to pull out chairs properly. She walked the remaining couple of steps to it, also with grace. She didn't toddle like a day-old colt.

Jean was pacing the front hall when I got home. She was beside herself. I watched her for a minute without saying anything. Finally, she glanced at me. "Where were you?" she asked. I told her I'd dropped by Jackson's place and then I'd gone to the real estate office to discuss selling some of Hannah's property. These were both things I had told Jean I would do. Jean told me that there wasn't anything having to do with Hannah's property that should keep me away from the house all damned day. That's what she said. All damned day.

"Gabrielle came today," said Jean. "From up the road."

"I know, Jean," I said. "She told us she'd drop by."

"But it wasn't Gabrielle," said Jean.

I laughed. "What do you mean it wasn't Gabrielle?" I asked.

"The woman said she was Gabrielle, but it wasn't her. It didn't look like her. It was Babette."

I righted one of the chairs we had in the front hall there and I sat in it. "You mean Babette who works at the ranch?" I asked. Then I sighed. "You're not talking sense. Let me make you something to eat. I'm tired, but let's go into the kitchen and I'll whip something up."

"Don't patronize me."

"Is that what I'm doing?"

"I'm sorry," said Jean, and she sighed. "This woman wants something. This woman calling herself Gabrielle. She's here for a reason. She might try to kill us."

Jean said she didn't want to go to the kitchen, but she followed me anyway. She was all riled up. Skittish. I sat at the kitchen table and thought about what we'd have for supper. Jean said she didn't want to sit when I offered. She stood and paced. Even as she related the events of her day, she paced. Jean said Gabrielle had shown up about fifteen minutes after I'd left, which Jean found strange. I asked her what was strange about it, and she said that Gabrielle showed up as if on schedule. It was as if she had been watching the house and waiting for me to leave. Jean said she knew it was Gabrielle when the doorbell rang. Jean approached the door, which had thick, glazed windows on either side of it as some older houses do. Hannah had wanted those put in because it reminded her of her mother's house before her mother had sold it. Jean said she could see a woman's beautiful silhouette briefly before she opened the door. The woman was walking, making circles in front of the door.

Jean opened the door just as the doorbell was rung a second time.

"Oh, pardon me," said Gabrielle as the door swung open. "I didn't realize you were standing there. Hi, Jean."

But Jean only looked at her without saying anything.

"It's me. Gabrielle. Remember, I live down the road? I promised I'd stop by. I mean, I told Kip that I would."

"What are you doing here?" Jean asked.

"I'm sorry?"

"You're not Gabrielle. You're Babette," said Jean.

"Pardon me?"

"You said your name was Gabrielle, but you're not Gabrielle. You're Babette."

"Jean, you're tired. I don't know what you mean. I don't know any Babette. Who's that?" And then Gabrielle laughed in a false, exaggerated way. At least that's how Jean described it. "Do you mind if I come in?"

Jean stood aside and Gabrielle came in. Jean got a better look at her. She was tall and womanly, and her hair was a dark shade of brown. Her eyes were also dark brown and sultry. Her most remarkable feature were her lips, which had a sensuous shape. They sometimes seemed almost to sneer, or so said Jean. Gabrielle's heels made a regular clack as she came in like horse hooves clopping.

"I think you forgot that you met me before," Gabrielle said.

"I didn't forget," said Jean. "But it wasn't you that I met."

"Oh, it wasn't me, was it?"

"Babette, what are you doing? Why would you want to play games with me?"

"It isn't any game. I told you that I'd stop by and here I am."

"Let me see your ID," Jean demanded.

Jean said she laid her palm out right in front of the lady. This forward kind of maneuver was out of place for someone like Jean.

"My ID?" Gabrielle asked.

"Yes, your identification. Your driver's license. You do have one, don't you?"

Gabrielle laughed again. "Of course, I have a driver's license," she said. She produced her license, which Jean told me very clearly displayed the woman's name. Gabrielle Delaney. And the image in the photo, though dark, as they typically are in driver's licenses, was distinctly that of the woman who now stood before her.

"Then your legal name is Gabrielle," Jean said. "You never were Babette. That was a rouse. You assumed a false identity."

Gabrielle didn't say anything. Jean attempted to read her face, but it was difficult to make out the meaning. The woman had become like a breed of horse that has assumed the characteristics of another breed. Gabrielle rest a hand on Jean's forearm, and Jean permitted her to. Gabrielle said: "Jean, let's go back to my house. I won't tell you what I think here, but we can talk there." Jean didn't agree to go. She didn't say anything. But she followed Gabrielle as they left the house. Jean made sure she had her house keys, and she locked the front door as she left. They got into Gabrielle's Chevy Impala and they drove to Gabrielle's house.

Gabrielle never glanced at Jean as they drove, Jean told me. She was attentive to the road. Her hands turned counterclockwise when the car needed to make a left. Her hands turned clockwise when the car needed to make a right. Gabrielle's foot hit the break when a dog sallied out into the street. The neighborhood was filled with semi-deserted houses. There were housewives who sat at home all day: tending to children that were too young for preschool. But most of the houses were derelict.

They came to Gabrielle's house: a one-story ranch house on a cul-de-sac. Jean noticed that there were new plantings in the yard: canopies from which vines twined. From across the street came the buzz of a lawnmower. The neighbor was riding it. He was mowing the lawn.

Jean followed Gabrielle into the house. "Would you like a glass of wine?" Gabrielle asked. Gabrielle took off the mantilla she had been wearing to reveal her soft, feminine shoulders. Gabrielle had been hiding her beautiful shoulders with her mantilla.

Jean declined the wine, but she later changed her mind. Gabrielle led Jean to the large kitchen, which was approached via a long corridor. They passed the living room of Shaker furniture, though they never went inside. The furniture looked plain, but that was the appeal of that kind of furniture. It was the kind of furniture that a rich person in Connecticut would have in their house, Jean told me. It was the sort of furniture that someone like Babette would have.

"Is this a fun game for you?" Jean asked when she reached the kitchen with Gabrielle.

Gabrielle didn't say anything. She was looking for the right bottle of wine and the corkscrew. Gabrielle found the corkscrew. It was sitting atop one of the green shelves in the pantry. Then she closed the pantry door and found a suitable bottle of wine. She uncorked the wine. Returning into the body of the kitchen, she found wine glasses. She poured wine into a pair of glasses and handed one to Jean. Jean didn't drink the wine right away. She was fighting for her life after all. She should have declined the wine glass, but she couldn't resist the well-shaped hands that had offered it to her. The hands were compelling like an animal's hairy, clawed paws. Gabrielle sipped from her own glass of wine and Jean followed suit. "You have beautiful hair," Gabrielle said. She raised her free hand to touch Jean's auburn mane.

Gabrielle would get a better look at this mane after she led Jean to her bedroom. It was a big room with double doors looking out onto the back lawn. The back lawn had a high fence so people driving on the road couldn't see in. They didn't know she had erected canopies and planted grapes to start a vineyard.

"I'm worried about you and Kip," Gabrielle said as the two women surveyed the vista. "I think your marriage may be in peril."

"Oh, is that what you think," said Jean.

"I want you to be comfortable here," said Gabrielle. "It's clear as day that you're not. One needn't be a clairvoyant to figure that out. Maybe you should do what I'm doing."

"And what is that?"

"Plant grapes," said Gabrielle, as if it was perfectly commonplace. "I'm starting a vineyard."

"You're not starting a vineyard."

"I am. Yes. I don't have a ton of land, but you can do something with four acres. You could start a vineyard even if you only had one acre, I think."

"Well, Kip, my husband, doesn't want a vineyard."

"How do you know?"

"Because he prefers horses," Jean said. "If we do anything at all, we'll get horses."

"Well, that's something after all," said Gabrielle.

"Besides, no one drinks wines from Texas."

Gabrielle grinned. "Not yet, but maybe one day they will."

"French vines won't grow here."

"There are other kinds of vines," said Gabrielle. "And I'm not sure it's true that French vines won't grow. We'll see."

Gabrielle found the dress she wanted to wear: a thin gauzy thing that was see-through at the top. A dress where someone looking at her would be able to make out her breasts completely. Their heft and their shape. With Jean standing behind her and watching her, Gabrielle unclasped the dress she wore at the shoulders and allowed it to fall to the ground. She stepped out of it and kicked it gingerly to a corner. She was naked. She turned briefly around to pull the cord of the overhead light, and Jean had a look at her. Her breasts were perky and the nipples were high-placed, like a young woman's. There was no sign of the effects of a viral disease, like that which Odette told people she suffered from. Gabrielle removed the dress she wanted from the hanger and lowered it down over her frame.

"Kip would never want to live on a vineyard," Jean said after Gabrielle was dressed.

"You should ask him," said Gabrielle. "You might be surprised."

"Are you suggesting that you know my husband better than I do?"

Gabrielle laughed then and Jean left soon after she finished her glass of wine. Jean left the wine glass in the kitchen and walked out of the house. Done relating to the story to me, Jean walked to the foot of the stairs. I followed her.

"What do you want to do?" I asked.

"We have to go," said Jean. "She's a crazy person. She's pretending to be someone else."

"Who do you mean? Gabrielle?"

"She's not Gabrielle," said Jean.

"But she showed you her driver's license."

Jean sighed. Her body was brimming with energy. She turned this-a-way and that-a-way. "Gabrielle. Babette. Whoever she is."

"You're not talking sense."

"I'm afraid," she said.

"Jesus," I said, beginning to walk up the stairs. The steps creaked and my boots made a heavy thud as they landed with each step.

"It's not just Babette," said Jean. "I've also been thinking about Odette."

"I thought you didn't want to talk about her. What, did she drive by in her Ford to harass you like before? Even though she's an invalid?"

"But that's the thing," said Jean. "I was doing some research. Kip, I don't think there's anything wrong with her. You said she has Schmallenberg, but that's not an illness that affects humans. It only plagues cattle."

"But she's an invalid," I told Jean. I was standing at the head of the stairs, and I turned to face Jean. "She has physical abnormalities. She can stand but she can barely walk. She takes two steps and she falls over."

"How can you be sure? Have you seen her arms and legs? She's always wearing long dresses. Dresses with those long, billowing arms like in the movies. For all we know, she's fine and just doesn't want to walk."

"Jean, stop," I told her. "First the Gabrielle thing and now this."

"Now what?"

"These conspiracy theories."

"What am I going to do if Babette comes back?"

"I don't know, Jean. What are you going to do?"

"I'm like a sitting duck here."

"A sitting duck?" I asked. "Really, Jean? Fine, take one of my guns. You can keep that .45 and I'll use the Python. You'll be fine as long as you hold onto that .45."

I returned to the bedroom. I unlocked the cabinet that I had given over to the storage of my guns. I had two of them.

There was my handy Colt .45 and the longer-necked, sexy Colt Python. I handed Jean the .45, though she wasn't of a mind to take it. Her fingers touched the cold surface of the metal lightly and then her hand, her body, began its gradual surrender. A horse surrenders after it's been broken. Jean turned away from me once she'd taken the gun. She descended the stairs and walked into the kitchen. I heard when she turned on the faucet and when she squeezed the dish-washing liquid out onto a sponge.

15

I heard Babette's shoes tapping up the stairs when I reached Odette's house. Babette had gotten back to the ranch before me. She'd gone up and I saw the imprint her Mary Janes left on the steps. The dust from the bottoms of her shoes. Babette was already talking to Odette when I reached the bedroom. Babette turned and paused when I entered the room. Odette struggled to sit up and the Colt rattled atop the surface of the table. Babette had her hair pinned up. She watched as I approached the foot of the bed.

"Has she lost her mind yet?" Odette asked.

"Not yet," Babette answered. "But she's close."

I smacked away the dried blood on the front of my jeans with a hand.

"It all seems so cruel," said Babette. "I don't understand why we have to do this."

"Oh, don't be ridiculous," said Odette, adjusting the lace collar of her dress. "Life isn't cruel. And it seems to me it'll be over soon."

"Life isn't cruel the heiress says," I muttered to myself, and then I turned to walk out of the room.

"I'm not done with you!" Odette yelled. Her voice took on a new, sudden violence. "Get your behind back here! Don't you dare walk away from me when I'm talking to you! How dare you? Where's my brand? You want to walk away from me? You're of a mind to turn away from me? You're nothing! Nothing at all!

You're nothing without me! Trash! That's what you are! Trash! Swishing away in your jeans like a bitch. I'll brand you. That's what I'll do. I'll brand my name on your ass!"

Odette adjusted herself in the bed. Babette took the wild-flowers she had picked and had been holding and left them atop the bedside table.

"That's what I'll do," Odette muttered, her hands trembling in excitement. "I'll take my brand and I'll brand my name right on your ass. Ha ha ha ha ha ha ha," she laughed.

I left the house unsteady as a day-old colt. It seemed Odette had pushed me and I'd fallen right into the dirt. My legs were shaky. I used a hand to smack away the blood and grime on the seat of my jeans, but there wasn't any. She hadn't actually pushed me. I regarded the ranch, suddenly alien, from the porch. Roping, branding, castrating. I saw Hunt astride a horse when I turned the bend in the Peugeot. A new mare I hadn't seen before.

16

"Good morning, Chantal," I said to Jean when I got up.

I stretched my arms out in a yawn and I threw my legs over the side of the bed. I turned to glance at Jean who had just then rolled over to face me. We watched the acres ranged out behind the house. There wasn't anything to see in the vista there. Max was still away on business, whatever his business was. I didn't remember. And the horse shed was silent and empty as the two horses that had lived in it had long since gone. I'd heard a man in the area had a mare that had birthed a new colt and I thought it'd be nice to get a colt in there. An overgrown field separated the empty horse shed from the house.

"I don't remember you coming back home," Chantal said.

"It was late," I said. "I didn't want to wake you, darlin'."

I stretched my torso out over Chantal and I swept away a wayward strand of her hair. I kissed her on the forehead. Then I stood up and walked to the closet. I removed the things that I had bought while I was away: the silk blouse, the fur-lined jacket and the high heels. These were all things that I knew Chantal liked. I removed the tags, so that Chantal wouldn't have to tear them off herself. Then I folded the clothes into a neat pile and left them on the edge of the bed. "I have to run to town, but I figured I'd help you get dressed," I told Chantal. She threw her legs over the side of the bed and stiffened her back

like a colt preparing to gallop for the first time. Chantal asked
me what drew me to town after she looked the clothes over.

"I have a box of steroids I need to sell," I told her. "I think I
know a guy in town who'll buy."

I was standing over the bureau, rummaging through the
drawer where I'd put the steroids.

"We don't need the money," Chantal said.

I turned around to look at her and I said: "I know we don't
need the money, but I figure it wouldn't hurt to have the cash.
Come here."

Chantal rose from the bed and walked over to where I was
by the bureau. I asked her to help me inject some winstrol
before I left. "No," she said. She had never said no to me before.
She had never said no to me about anything. I about-faced to
her since my back had been to her. Her look was sad. I thought
she needed encouragement. She was disoriented by my calling
her someone else's name. It wasn't my idea. So I smiled at
Chantal and brought her face close to mine. I kissed her: a
long, romantic type of kiss. That was just the encouragement
she needed. I pulled down the top of my jeans and the elastic
of my underwear, and Chantal positioned herself. She drew up
the steroid into the syringe from the bottle and she aimed it
perfectly over my left buttock. "No, do the right this time,"
I told her. Chantal changed position so she was standing on
the right of me. She aimed the point of the syringe perfectly
as before. She injected me. I felt the sharp of the needle slide
through the thin layer of fat that everyone has and then right
into the muscle. I wasn't fat myself. It's just that everyone has
some fat on their backside. The pain of the needle going in felt
good. It felt like I was in control even though I'd never been in
control. The touch of Chantal's hand was soft.

She still had some slick on her hands. Before I'd left
for Odette's, I'd helped Chantal with a clogged drain in the

kitchen. We used this device to pull up what was clogging the drain. Our hands were covered in this black oil by the time we were done. It was like the oil that lay beneath the land on Odette's ranch. The device didn't unclog the drain so I'd had to go to town to buy liquid drano.

Chantal walked away after shooting me up. She picked up the jacket that I'd left on the bed. She felt the lining of the jacket to see if it was real fur. If you have to ask you can't afford it. "I bet you need some money," I told Chantal. I pulled out my wallet, the expensive Italian leather wallet that Odette had given me for my birthday last year, and I removed a stack of twenties. There must have been $400 in twenties. I tossed them onto the bed like you would give money to someone you didn't care about. Like I would have given money to Chantal if I'd married her instead of Jean. "I know you love money," I said. It was a mean thing to say to Jean because she was the kind of person who would be happy in a world where there wasn't any money at all. I told her I needed to fill the tank in the Peugeot, but it was okay since I'd left some money in the car. I put on a flannel shirt and then I walked to the mirror to check how I was dressed.

Chantal followed me out into the hall. "I saw a man last night," she told me. I was halfway down the stairs, but I stopped in my tracks and turned to face her.

"What man?" I asked her.

"I don't know who he was," she said. "I went for a walk, all the way to the neighbor's house and behind a little bit. That's when I heard this dog barking in someone's yard. I turned around and there was a man walking toward me on the road. Well, it's not really a road. You've seen it. That narrow dirt road that runs behind all the houses here." She sighed. "Do you think it was Rob?"

"Rob?" I asked.

"Rob, the steroid-pusher."

"No, I don't think it was him. It's one of those convicts. There's a prison not far from here and sometimes a guy gets out. You know, escapes. Could be one of them."

"You can't be serious," said Chantal. "You never told me about the prison before."

"Sorry, Chantal," I said. "I must have forgotten."

"Why do you keep calling me that?" my wife asked. "You're trying to confuse me. I don't know why you would want to do that."

"I don't know what you're talking about," I said. I shrugged and continued walking down the stairs. "You know what to do if you get scared. That's what that gun is for."

"Please don't be away long."

But just before I got to the door, we heard the doorbell ring. I knew it was Gabrielle. "It's Gabrielle," I told Chantal. I walked the few remaining steps to the door. I opened it and there was Gabrielle.

"Sorry, guys," she said. "I remembered that I promised Chantal I'd drop off that dress. I know it's early, but I didn't see any reason not to come here first. I'm running errands today. Hi, Chantal. You look really nice today. Remember I promised to drop off this dress?"

"Chantal's worried about those men on the loose," I told Gabrielle. "The escaped convicts."

"Yeah, it's all over the news," Gabrielle said. "But it's nothing to be worried about," and she glanced quickly at Jean. The look Gabrielle gave Jean was feral. "I'm sure the police will catch the escapees before they murder anyone."

Gabrielle walked into the house as I walked out. She looked pretty today, but she smelled like cleaning solution. She smelled like she had been up all morning cleaning the kitchen. As I left the house, I looked back at the horse shed. I thought it'd be nice to have a horse in there, even if it was a colt or a yearling. But I was sure the man whose mare had birthed the colt had already sold it or promised it to someone.

I drove the Peugeot away from the house. As I drove, I thought that one day Jean would be nothing more than a footnote in my life and all because of Odette. She might have been more than that. I drove to Rob's house, which lay on the other side of town from where we were. When I reached Rob's, I was met with the unlikely scene of swans swimming in an artificial lake on the property. I supposed swans could settle anywhere. A swan is a creature capable of resurrecting itself. The house sat behind an electrified gate. I had to announce myself at a speaker. I announced myself, there was a scratch of static, and then I was buzzed in. Rob was alone. He had already opened the door for me. Rob was easy to spot because he was a foot taller than most people. Rob's penny loafers were the same color as the wood floor. Rob was pacing the living room at the back of the hall. He didn't notice the box of steroids I was carrying. He said that someone had broken into the house. I asked him how they could have gotten in with the gate up front. He told me he didn't know. He said: "That's what I get for letting whores into the house." I sat on the coach that faced a back window. That's when Rob noticed the steroids.

"If you want me to buy anything, you're out of your mind," he said. "These people just stole eight boxes."

"But there's always people around here looking to buy," I said. "All these juiced up guys."

Rob told me to follow him into the kitchen. He leaned his elbows against the laminate countertop. He was looking out the kitchen window. The kitchen was papered in green wallpaper showing riders chasing after deer.

"You're right. I can always use more product," Rob said.

There was the hum of a machine as Rob ran his water through a filtration system. He handed me the result in a glass when he was done. Rob turned to face me as he handed it to me. Rob was an old-fashioned sort of person and not as dangerous as people thought he was. He was just a survivor. He had a way of smiling and laughing with you even though he wasn't happy. Some men of the old school were like that. He stood and made small talk for a while. He watched me drink the water. Then he made a glass for himself. We heard the hum of the water filtration system again. Then Rob turned around and faced me as he drank his own glass of water. He was smiling and laughing again. I supposed it was his way of being polite.

Rob led me up to the second floor. His house was unusually large and grand for where we were. He had just bought it with roid money. A double staircase with a walnut railing swept up to the second floor. But there was still the Texas dust which had settled in the cracks on the staircase planks. The dust could be seen under the strong light of the chandelier. Rob's bedroom was the last room at the end of a long hall. The room was part of a suite. There was the bedroom, the walk-in-closet as large as another bedroom, and the bathroom. There was a vanity mirror in the bedroom. I set the box down atop the brown marble countertop after we walked in. I opened the box with the pocketknife I always carried with me. A switchblade. Switchblades used to be known as spring blades or Springers because of the spring type of operation they used. When the box was opened, I turned around and showed Rob the open container with its contents. Rob said I looked like I wanted to shoot up, and I did. He had syringes. Tearing open the plastic of a syringe and undoing the safety aluminum of a vial from the box, I drew the steroid compound into a syringe. Rob walked toward me to help me. I heard a horse chuffing outside.

Rob had horses roaming the grounds. He had a worker to help him on the property too. I didn't ask him if he thought the worker had something to do with the recent theft. I handed Rob the prepared syringe and he injected me. His hands were rough. After I pulled up my pants, Rob sat on the edge of his bed. I told him I had another box of steroids at home that I could sell. I bought most of my product from Rob but not all of it. I had been sourcing from him for a couple years. "All right, I'll buy," Rob said. He had done well for himself. Well enough that he could buy a property like this even if it was out in the middle of nowhere.

Rob paid more than the steroids were worth. I saw a framed picture near the bed as I was walking out. It was the image of a tanned woman under the arm of a much larger man.

Rob said: "You didn't know I used to be married, did you? You never know how things will turn out. She wanted to get married in this old-fashioned wedding dress. We had to pick it up from a specialty shop on the East Coast. We had to get it altered. It was the kind of dress that's not really white, but off-white. Not the kind of white a virgin would wear. But I think people know the color is supposed to be white when they see the lace: the lace collar and all that. We had an engagement party and all that. She invited all of her friends. I invited all of my friends. I had a lot of friends back then. We were married for two years. She left me for another guy, and then the guy made up these stories about all the horrible things I had done to her. People always slander you after they hurt you."

I turned round to look at Rob because I didn't realize he had been married and it was out of character for him to say something deep. I left the bedroom. As I left the house, I watched the scene outside the front windows. The house had a clearing in front of it. The horses grazed on the clearing. This had once been forested land, but the settlers cleared the land when they setup ranching and brought ranching culture. Rob had left the television on in the living room. On it played one of those action movies "for men who like movies." I only caught half a minute of it. It was the kind of movie where people smuggle drugs from one city to another, hounded by the police and rival gangs. There's a big party in the middle when the men are at the top of their game and free from their pursuers. But they always die in the end. There's always a beautiful girl in a fur coat that the male lead falls in love with.

I took the 120 to get back home. I usually avoided the main roads for the unpaved ones, but I wanted to get back fast. When I reached the house, I saw that the Jeep belonging to our neighbor Max was parked down the road in front of his house. I made out a tall man, a giant, standing in his yard as I neared the house. I knew it was Max. The front door to Hannah's house was open. It was nighttime now. I walked into the house and entered the hall. I tried to avoid the pools of blood on the floor, but I got blood on the soles of my boots anyway. I realized it later when I took them off. I was holding my wallet in my hands as I walked in. It was fat with the money that Rob had paid me for the steroids.

I neared the living room where the switched-on television played. I felt a shock through my body when I touched the TV monitor to switch it off. I felt Jean's sadness in the room. I found Jean in the kitchen. I stepped over Jackson's body at the threshold into the kitchen, and I called out her name. "Jean," I said. I didn't have to call her Chantal anymore as I had already accomplished what Odette wanted. "Jean, we can't sit in here," I told her. I told her we should go the living room and wait for the police to come. I'd call them up on the phone. Jean gave me a helpless look and reached out for my hand. She had a bruise on her forearm, but she never told me what it was from. The bruise was large and it seemed to grow in the time that we waited for the police to show. Jean had to be careful because of her hemophilia. When the police came, I'd have to tell them to take her to the hospital so she could get a transfusion of plasma with the coagulation factors that she needed. People with hemophilia lack the coagulation factors which allow their blood to clot properly. Hemophilia is usually passed through families on the X chromosome, but it can also occur as a spontaneous mutation. Jean's father was a hemophiliac and her mother was a carrier. It was a one-in-a-million occurrence for these two unknowns to meet one another and have a hemophiliac daughter. Outside the house, the linden trees had narrow, swaying bodies.

My boots made a loud tap as I walked into the living room. Jean followed me. I pulled out a chair for her to sit. Jean told me that she thought Jackson was the man who'd followed her earlier so she shot him. A man had come to the door and she didn't know it was Jackson. It had been dark. I swept Jean's auburn hair away from her face as she told her story. A tress had fallen over her face. I told her I'd put a cup of coffee on and then I'd call the police. I took Jean's hand before I turned to leave for the kitchen again and she had blood on her fingers. She hadn't lost her beauty, but she looked pained. I called the police. I turned the coffeemaker on and put the coffee in. Then I waited with Jean in the living room. We both turned when we heard the police car tires turning into the driveway.

17

I was met at the door to the ranch manager's house by Hunt who hugged me in his warm way. He was holding a bottle of Jack. The mouth of the bottle pressed against my back when he hugged me. Then he returned to the kitchen. I heard the thud of his hobnailed boots. Hunt had a thick mustache now and looked more like a man than before. He was joined in the kitchen by Esteban, who was the cowboy that I'd hired to do the work while I was away. Odette hadn't filled the ranch manager position. She seemed to think that I'd always return. Hunt said something and Esteban laughed. Esteban had an easygoing manner, which was an important quality in a cowboy newly hired on a place, especially if he was expected to work directly with the owner. The owners were often strange. When I'd first met Esteban, I'd sat with him on the bluffs over the river and he told me about the wife and children he'd left back home.

Hunt turned to face me and I saw that he'd opened the first four buttons of his button-down shirt. I knew that meant he planned to go out to town, since that was how he attired himself when he did. He wore an enormous cowboy hat that I hadn't seen before. After he'd gone, the ranch was silent. I saw the Peugeot I'd parked on the front lawn. The police had allowed me to take the Peugeot with me as they didn't consider it evidence. Nothing had happened in the Peugeot. I noticed the empty spaces of the ranch: the gap between the ranch manager's house and Odette's house. There was the well-worn path that led from the stable to the barn. The path remained well-worn from the days when this had been a more active place. Hunt returned to the ranch late in the night. He'd come back for his Smith & Wesson. He'd left it in his room. He said there were all kinds of strangers in town and it looked like it was going to be a rowdy night. Rowdy didn't mean the same thing to Hunt as it did to me. I was older and had seen more things. He mentioned Odette and said that she'd be glad I'd returned. He said: "I think you should be careful there, Kip. Some bulls you just need to back off from." Then he poured himself a glass of water to sober up.

"Well, I think you should mind your own business," I told him.

"What?" he asked.

"I said mind your own business. It's no business of yours what I do or don't do with the owner."

Hunt marched over to me. He looked me over for a second and then he shoved me hard. My back hit the wall paneling with a loud smack. After I righted myself, I caught up with Hunt. I tried to trip him as he walked away. He stumbled, but he caught himself before falling. I walked to Odette's house after Hunt and Esteban had gone. I could hear the boys' happy talk in the truck as Esteban drove off. The door to the house was unlocked as it was always kept unlocked. In the living room, I sat down to loosen my bootlaces and noticed the blood caked on the soles. I took the boots off. I didn't want to track blood and innards into the house. I was soon glad I'd taken them off. My feet ached as if I'd walked a long road and had finally stopped. I thought of going to the kitchen and making myself a drink. Drinking was a rare thing for me to do since I knew that calories from alcohol were the worst kind. Alcohol carried seven kilocalories per gram, which were calories that your body had no use for whatsoever. The wind picked up and I heard the tree branches smacking against the window.

I walked toward the kitchen. My steps didn't make a sound as my feet were unshod. Beside the kitchen was the closet of things that had belonged to the previous girls. I removed a ring of six keys from my pocket. I took the longest of the keys: a stern iron rod with three wards. I pushed this into the keyhole. The door swung open and I entered the closet. Sitting atop a table by the wall were the photos of all the girls. They were Tiffany, Tallulah and Charlotte. Charlotte had been unspeakably pretty, but she wasn't quite like Jean. I removed the folded-in-half Polaroid of Jean from my wallet. The expensive leather wallet that Odette had given me for my birthday. I added Jean's picture to the bunch and walked out of the room. I used the iron key of three wards to lock the closet again. A window in the hall looked out onto the tornado-scarred land.

When I reached the kitchen, I rifled through the kitchen cabinets for a bottle of Jack. I didn't find any. It seemed I wouldn't have that drink after all. Then I heard the rapid, happy patter of feet racing down the stairs. It was the elated patter of a beautiful woman running to me. My heart pounded in my chest. I turned to face the sound. I tensed the muscles in my chest and shoulders. I wished I had time to shoot myself up with steroids, but it was too late. She was already here. Odette appeared at the kitchen doorway wearing a low-cut dress. The hem of the dress fell below her knees. The hem of the dress seemed to sway happily when she walked like when a woman dances with a man she likes. Odette's face was a forest of many seductive shadows. She slowed her pace as she neared me. I placed a hand on her narrow slip of a waist when she reached me. She placed a hand on my chest. She said: "I'm well again. We can go away like I always wanted." We'd go far from the ranch and away from all the things I had known.

Roping, branding, castrating. I continued to hold onto Odette's waist and she glanced out of a window. In the distance, the pumpjacks were finally set in motion again. They beat against the angry earth, and when the oil sprung forth from the ground the faces of the workers were splattered with it. Odette had resumed oil production on her great-granddaddy's land.

A feral horse had wandered onto the land. We saw it lower its head as it halted in the field behind the house. There was the occasional feral horse in the area. The horse spotted us. It was sleek and muscular. Its gait was correct in spite of its being feral. It seemed to dance in the window. Odette laughed. It was the laugh of the oilman who knew there would never be a time when oil wouldn't be needed. There would never be a place.

Coming soon from Alexey Williams

JEFFREY THE DWARF